OUT OF CONTROL: KAT'S STORY

"The lawyer and I had a date on Thursday night." *Where had that come from?*

"Really? Where did you go—a lecture at the law school or a porn film at the Third Avenue Theatre?"

"Stop." She hit his arm again. "We had drinks and dinner at The Desmond."

"Did he spring for a room or did you just neck in the back seat of his car?" It was said laughingly, but there was a tightening around Zack's mouth as he darted a glance over at Kat.

Her face was flaming now, even in the cool breeze that had come up as the sun was setting. She hugged herself, as though chilled. Zack put his arm around her, rubbing her shoulder as if to warm her. Kat turned into him and whispered into his ear, "He got a room."

Zack's fingers dug into her shoulder but his voice remained calm, almost disinterested.

"Was he any good?"

"What kind of a question is that?" Kat demanded.

His eyes on the game, he replied, "Well, I'm thinking it's the first time in almost ten years that you've gotten any, and I was hoping he'd be good enough to have made it worth the wait."

There was a long pause, before Kat whispered in his ear again. "It was worth the wait."

Copyright © 2016, Deborah Sabin
Out of Control: Kat's Story
Books > Fiction Romance > Romance Novels
Keywords: romance, erotica, bondage, domination, submission, Alpha males, second chance

Trade Paperback ISBN: 978-1-54101-553-1
Print Release: March 2017

Editing and Interior Format by Deelylah Mullin
Cover Design by Kris Norris

All rights reserved. The unauthorized reproduction or distribution of this copyrighted work, in whole or part, by any electronic, mechanical, or other means, is illegal and forbidden.

This is a work of fiction. Characters, settings, names, and occurrences are a product of the author's imagination and bear no resemblance to any actual person, living or dead, places or settings, and/or occurrences. Any incidences of resemblance are purely coincidental.

MORGAN MALONE

Out of Control:
Kat's Story

MORGAN MALONE

DEDICATION

To MLH. Always.

ACKNOWLEDGEMENTS

Nothing I write would see the light of day without the encouragement and support of my writing group, Writing Women's Minds (Maggie, Posey and Sharon); my beta-readers, Sue W. and Sue G.; and my fabulous editor, Deelylah Mullin. Thank you, thank you, thank you.

TABLE OF CONTENTS

CHAPTER ONE	1
CHAPTER TWO	24
CHAPTER THREE	38
CHAPTER FOUR	50
CHAPTER FIVE	63
CHAPTER SIX	70
CHAPTER SEVEN	83
CHAPTER EIGHT	89
CHAPTER NINE	106
CHAPTER TEN	111
CHAPTER ELEVEN	122
CHAPTER TWELVE	130
CHAPTER THIRTEEN	138
CHAPTER FOURTEEN	154

CHAPTER FIFTEEN	**161**
CHAPTER SIXTEEN	**170**
DEAR READER	**175**
ABOUT MORGAN MALONE	**177**
TAKING CONTROL: RICK'S STORY	**179**

CHAPTER ONE

Curiosity killed the cat. Katarina's Russian-born grandmother said it all the time, usually with a raised eyebrow and a glance toward Katarina.

Yes, but satisfaction brought her back, Katarina snickered to herself. Sometimes.

Gripping the steering wheel of her car, she rolled her head from shoulder to shoulder to get out some of the kinks. Kinks. She smiled. Thank God for friends like Zack. Friends with benefits. Well, not *those kind of benefits.* She loved her *dates* with Zachary Reichman, only they really weren't dates. Zack, her best male friend, took her to dinner, ball games, and family affairs. And he gave marvelous back rubs. They loved each other but weren't in love, liked each other with an easy affection stretching back over a decade, and she respected the legal abilities that made Zack a powerful litigator. Zack had been best friends with Michael Kaufman, Kat's husband, long before Kat met them. She could never tell who cried the most that night ten years earlier when she told Zack that Michael had been killed in the Iraqi War; their tears soaked each other's clothes until they were sodden with sadness.

Now, Kat and Zack spent so much time together many of their colleagues assumed they were a couple. But, they weren't. Why weren't they, Kat wondered, the kink in her neck back again, why weren't they more than friends?

Don't go there, she muttered to herself, and directed her attention back to the traffic. Normally, Katarina was not out on the highway in the middle of the day. Her specialty was appellate work; she wrote brilliant briefs on appeals. Most of her days were spent in her glass walled office, hunched over her computer, law books piled on her desk and files spread across her worktable.

But, not today. Her secretary's niece had gotten a speeding ticket on the arterial and had come to her for help. While it was out of her area of expertise, Kat had agreed to make a few calls to try to reduce the points for the ticket. The niece was tearfully grateful even though Katarina had been unable to make any promises. The Town Attorney for the court with jurisdiction over that section of the highway was not someone she recognized, but regardless, she had made the call to his office yesterday.

The deep voice that greeted her had caused a quiver of excitement down in her belly.

"Ms. Galchinsky, what can I do for you today?"

After hearing his smoky, sexy, drawl, Kat had a number of ideas about what he could do for her and what she could do for him. But none were appropriate for a plea arrangement telephone conference.

"Well, Mr. Robbins, you can get this ticket kicked for me. My client had a violently ill husband in the car with her and was trying to get him to the ER when she was pulled over for doing eight miles over the speed limit."

"Hmm, I don't see anything in the supporting deposition about an ER situation."

"I can fax you a copy of the ER admissions form. The husband had food poisoning and was there for six hours."

"Listen, why don't you drop it by sometime this week? If it is in order, we can sign off on a plea agreement, and I'll recommend it to Judge Main at Traffic Court on Thursday."

He was a bit high-handed, Kat thought, but if she could get the ticket dismissed for Cecilia's niece, she'd put up with it. Poor little Town Attorney—with the sexy as hell voice—flexing his muscles.

"I'm not going to be in Waterford anytime this week, counselor." If Kat had her way, she would never be in Waterford for any legal work. She didn't even know where the damn Traffic Court was located.

"That's fine. I don't use the Town offices that often. You could come by my office in Albany, if that is more convenient." He gave her a very prestigious address in a classy office park not far from her own office building.

"I have a luncheon meeting tomorrow near you. I could meet with you around two, if that works."

"That will be fine. I'll see you tomorrow, Ms. Galchinsky."

So, there Katarina was at a quarter to two tooling along I-90 in her red Volvo on her way to meet an innocuous Town Attorney with a kick-ass voice and a blue-ribbon office. She had done her homework and checked out his firm's website online. He was a named partner, the son and grandson of local judges, specializing in commercial and contract law. *What the hell was he doing as Town Attorney for a small town, handling traffic tickets and zoning appeals?*

As she sang along with the music blaring from her car radio, Kat recalled that the picture on the law firm's home page had revealed just the head of a nice-looking man, mid-40s, dark hair, dark eyes and a dimple. Beyond that and the whiskey-deep voice, she couldn't explain why she had just spent fifteen minutes in the ladies' room freshening up after her lunch appointment with Mia, her best girlfriend from law school. Mia had even commented that something must be up when Katarina pulled a small atomizer of Lolita Lempicka out of the large Louis Vuitton tote that was both her purse and her briefcase.

"You never wear the good stuff on work days, Kat. What's up?"

Kat shook back her mane of auburn curls and smiled her Cheshire cat smile. "What makes you think something is up? Maybe I wore this perfume for you, girlfriend. I know how much you like it."

"Yeah, I like it on me. It just isn't the same on you. But, it's a man-killer and you know it, so who are you meeting next, counselor?" Mia was not chief trial counsel for a major insurance company for nothing.

"I'm meeting some Town Attorney to plead down a ticket for my secretary's niece. You probably don't know him... Sam Robbins?"

Mia had the grace to look surprised and then her brown eyes narrowed. She leaned back against the vanity and peered closely at Kat, taking in every detail.

Avoiding her friend's inquisitive stare, Kat looked in the broad mirror, trying to see herself as Mia was seeing her. As Sam Robbins might see her. She was wearing her unruly red hair loose, instead of pulled back in the usual French braid. And, instead of her traditional pearls, she had diamond studs in her ears and another diamond dangling on a long chain just above the cleavage of her red silk blouse. Edgy but still professional and proper. Well, almost proper.

"I know him. He's hot." Mia's voice had an almost lustful tone.

Kat was a bit taken aback. Mia had been happily married for several years to Steve, a cuddly nuclear physicist, the quintessential absent-minded professor. But, Kat knew and admired Mia's still excellent *hottie radar*.

"What do you mean, he's hot? Do you mean he's a stud or do you mean his career is on fire?"

"Both." Mia grinned as a faint flush crept up her friend's exquisite cheekbones. "He comes from political royalty around here, and word is that he will be the next County Judge.

And, he is one fine-looking specimen." Mia licked her lips, adding emphasis.

Kat paused in applying gloss to her full lips and glanced at her friend. Mia was tiny and dark, her Italian heritage readily apparent in her olive complexion, chocolate brown eyes and short black hair. They had been friends since the first day of law school and provided the perfect foil for one another.

While Kat was not tall at five foot six, she had several inches on Mia. And Kat was not thin; her frame was strong and well made. Add to that her high Slavic cheekbones and improbable violet eyes: Kat herself had often been referred to as a *hottie*. She usually kept her fiery hair in check, her Liz Taylor eyes hidden behind tortoise shell glasses and her lush body concealed in conservatively cut, dark business suits. Today, however, she was wearing her contacts and had chosen a light khaki suit over a V-neck cherry blouse and linen Manolo Blahnik open-toed pumps—her bright red toenails peeping out.

"Well, Katarina, whatever you have in mind, and I have my own suppositions about that, make sure he signs the damn plea agreement before you engage in…more complex negotiations."

Picking up her designer bag, Mia pushed open the door of the ladies' room and strode out, with a sputtering Kat following behind her. Mia turned to Kat as they went through the front door of the restaurant and added, "But, either way, I want details! Steve has been on a business trip all week, and I need some really good stuff, even if it is second-hand." Mia climbed into her suburban-mom SUV.

Opening the door to her Volvo, Kat turned and laughingly retorted, "Yeah, I'll be sure to tell you all about the way I'm going to badger him into dismissing the charge after I show him pictures of the vomit all over my client's jeans—courtesy of the little delay caused by his overzealous cops. He's just lucky we're not suing for the dry-cleaning and car-detailing expense."

"You should at least threaten him with that, if your other strategy doesn't work." Mia tossed out before she pulled onto Central Avenue and headed downtown.

Kat was still smiling about her friend's wiseass remarks a few minutes later when she parked in the shaded lot adjacent to the sleekly modern office building. Robbins, Robbins, Greenleaf and Mineaux, LLP had the entire third floor. She checked her lip gloss one more time, left her sunglasses on the front seat and strode purposefully into the pale marble interior of the lobby. Putting thoughts of Mr. Robbins and his dimple aside, she mentally reviewed the rest of her busy afternoon during the brief elevator ride. A discreet chime snapped her back to the present when the elevator doors opened into a spacious reception area. Kat's high heels clicked on the polished wooden floor before they sank into the thick Oriental carpet centered before a large mahogany desk. A trim, gray-haired woman smiled upon hearing Ms. Galchinsky was there to see Mr. Robbins, stood, and ushered Kat down the wide hall to a large conference room, assuring Kat Mr. Robbins would be in to see her directly.

"We all have the same damn conference rooms," Kat muttered to herself as she surveyed the room. Twelve burgundy leather chairs marched around the perimeter of the large mahogany table, anchored by a heavy armchair at each end. The requisite screen for video displays hung on the far wall, bracketed by a bookcase and a console, holding the electronics. The soft green walls were hung with hunt scenes interspersed between portraits of the firm's founders, all framed in gilt and mahogany. Everything was subtly aristocratic and rich, as befitted a firm established over one hundred years earlier. The conference room in Kat's office contained all the same accoutrements and the requisite twelve-foot long table, though her offices had a distinct Asian flare, with black lacquer, painted silk screens and bamboo plants in antique blue and white vases, all courtesy of the senior partner's wife's travels to the Far East every year or so.

She didn't have more time than it took to tap her short red nails impatiently once or twice on the polished surface of the table before the door opened, and there he was. Damn. Sam Robbins was a hottie.

"Sorry to have kept you waiting, Ms. Galchinsky." A tanned, long-fingered hand was extended to her. Her eyes fastened on that hand, with the firm yet gentle grip. There was a delay in releasing her hand that extended for just a few seconds beyond a proper business handshake. She glanced quickly up at his face. Oh, yeah, he knew what he was doing. Kat had been pretty much out of the loop with men since Michael died, except for Zack, and Zack didn't count that way because she knew him so well. There was no flirting between them, more comfort given and received than anything else, but she still knew when a man was hitting on her. And Sam Robbins was definitely hitting on her. How inappropriate. And delicious.

"Not a problem, Mr. Robbins. It was only a minute." She finally looked into his eyes. They were a deep green—darker than emeralds—and fringed with short, thick eyelashes. His black hair was liberally sprinkled with silver at the temples and swept back from his angular face. As he stepped around her and laid his file at the end of the polished table, she realized how tall and toned he was. His shoulders were broad under the fine cotton of his starched white business shirt, his wrists graceful beneath the monogrammed cuffs and subtle gold cufflinks.

And his ass looked tight, covered by the light gray flannel trousers.

Sam pulled out the chair for her. Katarina sank gracefully into the cool leather, grateful to be at eye-level with him when he took the armchair at a right angle to her. His long legs crossed at the knee and she admired the deep cordovan leather of his tasseled loafer and the intricate pattern on his gray socks. She was a sucker for argyle socks on men. She was fast becoming a sucker for that lean, yet muscled, thigh upon which he rested one hand, the other flipping open the manila case folder. He was hot.

"Well, this seems pretty straightforward, Ms. Galchinsky. Your client was driving above the speed limit, albeit less than ten miles over the limit. I think we can reduce this to a lesser included offense, say, parking on the pavement."

He looked up at her with an almost smug smile playing across his wide mouth.

Oh, yeah, I'll bet you get most people to just fall right into line with that supreme self-confidence and that killer grin. Not me, bucko.

"I agree, Mr. Robbins, that the case is pretty simple." Kat let a small sweet smile pass across her lips.

"My client was going eight miles over the speed limit in an attempt to get her extremely ill husband to the Emergency Room. Rather than escort her to the ER, your police officer held her up for over fifteen minutes while he ran her license and wrote out a ticket before giving her a lecture about speeding. Her husband was in the ER for hours; she incurred over a hundred dollars in expenses getting the car cleaned after her husband vomited all over it in the ER parking lot. That is the mess that could have been avoided if your officer had taken the time to assess the gravity of my client's situation, and offer her assistance, instead of harassing her."

Kat leaned in for the kill. "You guys a little hard up for municipal funds over there in Waterford? What's the ticket quota up to this month?"

Katarina watched with some amusement as a flush crept up his tanned neck to his patrician cheekbones. Before he could sputter an answer, she flipped open the file she had removed from her bag and pushed several glossy eight-by-ten colored photos across the table so he could view the disgusting mess that covered the interior of her client's compact car.

"I think we can both agree that this ticket should be dismissed in the interest of justice, counselor." Katarina concluded, a little queasy herself from looking at the pictures.

Her adversary was getting a little pale. He pushed the photos into his file.

"Of course, I will have to discuss this with the judge, but I will request that the matter be dealt with leniently given the circumstances." The killer grin was gone, but there was evidence of a dimple just at the corner of his mouth.

"I appreciate that, Mr. Robbins, and you might add that the cleaning bills would be more than any fine that the court could legitimately impose in this matter." Kat closed the file and slid it back into her bag. "My client, of course, will not pursue reimbursement if the ticket is dismissed."

"You aren't threatening me, are you, Ms. Galchinsky?" He had the grace to smile.

"I would not dream of it, counselor. Just pointing out the options." Kat smiled, too. It was not often that she engaged in settlement negotiations anymore, but she still enjoyed the back-and-forth.

Sam stood, towering over her. As she reached for her bag, he leaned over and cupped her elbow in his hand, as if to help her to rise. Kat stood, with her bag in one hand, his hand still holding her elbow.

"If you don't mind me saying, you pack quite a punch for the little bit of a thing that you are, Ms. Galchinsky." A seductive smile played across his lips, deepening his sexy dimple. Kat had the fleeting impression he could turn that smile on and off in an instant, whenever he felt the need to use it to get his way. She could feel the heat of his touch through the sleeve of her jacket.

It seemed his fingers lingered overlong on her arm, and she could've sworn he was lightly stroking the inside of her elbow with his thumb. There were ripples of excitement radiating through her. Involuntarily, she sighed. Looking up at him through her lashes, she could see his pupils flare as the soft sound escaped her lips. Sam leaned in just as she stepped back.

"What the hell?" He glared at her and then grinned, as if he knew just how close she had been to succumbing to him.

Katarina was sure that he had been about to kiss her. She had felt the pull and almost reached for him before her good sense came to her rescue. Not while she had a case still pending with him, no way.

She saw Sam's green eyes rake her, from head to toe. Her eyes widened and her nipples were pinpoints against the red silk of her blouse. Kat softly chewed on her full bottom lip. She found herself wishing Sam were plying the swollen flesh with his teeth. That unbidden thought had her take another step away from him.

"I will wait for your call about the plea arrangements, Mr. Robbins. I assume I don't need to appear at court next Monday."

"No need to appear there, Ms. Galchinsky. You can come back here once I have the Judge's signature on the dismissal of the charge." He moved to the conference room door and opened it, motioning for her to precede him into the hall.

She had the grace to smile at his capitulation. When she reached the doorway, Kat extended her hand to shake his. He clasped her hand in both of his. His firm grip said everything: *You may have won this battle, counselor, but the spoils of war are coming to me.*

"I look forward to speaking with you, Mr. Robbins." Kat almost reluctantly withdrew her hand from his possessive grasp.

"I look forward to our next meeting...Kat." His smile was pure challenge.

He held the main door for her, his hand firmly on her back as he guided her to the elevator. She had the distinct impression of being toyed with, like a cat with a mouse. Except this time, she was the prey. Kat stepped into the elevator and turned back to him, smiling very carefully. As the doors closed, she whispered, "Until the next time, Sam."

Nothing untoward had happened, and it looked like she was getting her client's ticket dismissed, so why was she so pissed? Kat was fuming as she sped along the highway to her office. In the midst of prioritizing the work that waited for her back in her office, she felt overwhelmed by a sense of anger and frustration and it was all directed at Sam Robbins.

He just rubs me the wrong way. Well, no, he didn't rub me at all. Except for that electrically charged lingering touch while he was holding onto her elbow—and what was that all about? Otherwise, he had done nothing more than shake her hand. And that nothing was it, she reasoned. There had seemed to be so much more, just there under the surface of everything he said, every look he cast her way, every touch.

He thinks he is in control here but he has another think coming. I am in control. I am always in control.

The only daughter of her parents, the only granddaughter of her immigrant grandmother, first in her family to go to college, Kat had been in control for decades. She handled the legal issues for the family: her parents' delicatessen, her grandfather's estate, and her brothers' too frequent parking tickets. As a widow, she made every decision affecting her life and had for over ten years. She had no one to answer to, no one to consult, and no one to turn to for a decision or even an opinion. Even at her law firm. As a partner, Kat did not have to arrange for Secretary's Day presents and birthday celebrations, but she did. She could have passed Cecilia's niece's ticket on to an associate to handle, but she didn't. She was on the hiring committee, the promotion committee and the management committee. If she controlled every detail of her life and everyone around her, then no harm would come to anyone. No one else would die.

A sob caught in her throat. Michael would still be alive if she had been in control, she thought. After September 11, Michael had wanted to join the Army. She had tried to dissuade him but to no avail. She succeeded only to the point of urging him to join JAG, the Judge Advocate General's Corp, and not the Infantry, assuming lawyers wouldn't go into a war zone. Fat lot of good that had done! Once through Officer's Training, Michael was posted to Iraq. He was killed by an IED while travelling to meet with a soldier who was under investigation. He had come home in pieces, and she had not been able to protect him.

Kat pulled into her parking spot and just sat. With the engine running and Tchaikovsky playing, a startling realization came to her. *I am so sick and tired of always being in control. I am so tired of making every damn decision. God, I just want someone strong enough to tell me what to do and then make me do it.*

Stunned a chance encounter with a hot stranger had sent such unexpected emotions and desires swirling through her with such intensity, Kat took several deep breaths to calm down.

She checked her face in the car's rearview mirror. Rubbing the traces of unshed tears from her eyes, Kat pulled herself together, as she always did, as she had always done, and resolved to put Sam Robbins and his cocky attitude out of her mind.

⁓

The plea agreement arrived at her office a few days later. Kat was loath to admit to herself she had hoped Sam would call her to pick it up or, even better, drop it off himself.

Cecilia's niece came by the office to sign the papers. The young schoolteacher could not seem to find the words to express her gratitude that the ticket would be dismissed "in the interest of justice" without any points on her license or any fine. Cecilia opined, "No Town Attorney was any kind of a match for Kat's awesome legal skills."

Shooing them out of her office, Kat dialed Sam's number. Denying to herself that she just wanted to hear that whiskey voice again, Kat was disappointed nonetheless when the receptionist informed her Mr. Robbins was on another line. Kat told his secretary the plea agreement had been signed and was about to ask if it should be mailed to Mr. Robbins directly or to the Town Court Clerk.

"Hello, Ms. Galchinsky." Sam's voice was suddenly on the line. "You can mail the signed papers to either address.

Kat's heart fluttered at the sound of his voice even as it plummeted at the realization she probably would not be seeing him again.

Until Sam continued, "Or, you could drop the papers off here, if you are going to be near the office anytime today. I will be heading over to Town Court for this evening's traffic docket around six tonight, and I can bring them with me."

She had not a single reason in the world to be out of her office, but Kat found herself telling him she could stop by on her way back from an appointment around four o'clock that afternoon.

This time Sam met her at the receptionist's desk. The polite handshake he gave Kat felt like a caress. Sam led her back, not to the conference room, but to his large office at the end of a long hallway.

"This was my father's office before he was elected to the bench. It is a little smaller than the office I was using, but I like it because it is out of the way and so very quiet." Sam motioned her into the wood-paneled room that looked out on the adjacent nature park. Furnished in dark wood and burgundy leather, Sam's office matched his conference room. Kat thought it could easily have been situated in a centuries-old brownstone on Elk Street and not a modern office building in a corporate park. As if he were reading her mind, Sam remarked the law firm moved from a downtown location as the practice grew, but his father had insisted all the original furnishings be kept.

Kat was skittish, just like a long-tailed cat in a room of rocking chairs, as her grandmother would say. Dropping her bag on one of the leather chairs facing Sam's mahogany desk, she rummaged through it for the case folder. Sam leaned against the desk, crossed his ankles and seemed to be watching her with a bemused smile on his face. Kat licked her lips as she handed him the papers. She noticed that Sam jolted a bit when her tongue slid over her lowerlip.

Their fingers brushed and again Kat felt that charge. He was so incredibly handsome, tall and dark, lean and elegant in his tailored white shirt, regimental striped tie and navy blue trousers. Her eyes swept down to the tasseled wingtip loafers he wore and she smiled at the red and navy striped socks revealed below the cuff of his pants. Her eyes trailed back up his long legs, pausing appreciatively at the bulge at the juncture of his thighs. She sighed and then met his eyes.

"I think everything is in order here. I will just file these papers tonight when I go to court." He had barely glanced at the file before he placed it behind him on his desk.

Curiosity got the better of her. "Why ever are you the Town Attorney there? This is such a huge practice, why do you do traffic court?"

"We originally lived in Waterford, years ago. Lawyers from my family have been the Town Attorney there for decades. It's like a rite of passage. And it doesn't require much of my time."

"I see." Kat bent to gather up her bag. "Well, thank you for taking care of this matter so promptly. My client was very pleased with the outcome, as was my secretary. She runs my office, so it is important for me to keep her happy. So, thank you again." Kat started to turn toward the door until Sam's deep voice stopped her. She looked back at him. Sam was still leaning against the desk, but even with his relaxed pose, he seemed to have become more alert, more aware of her every move.

"Ms. Galchinsky, would you agree that this matter is concluded? The filing of the plea acceptance is just a formality, wouldn't you say?" His voice felt like a caress along her goose-bumped skin.

Kat nodded her head; a few wisps of auburn curls escaping from the ponytail neatly bowed low on her neck. She straightened, her full breasts straining against the navy linen dress she wore, her nipples hardening to sharp points, under his heated stare.

"Good. That's what I thought, too. Could you come over here?" Sam's voice crackled with authority, and with pleasure.

She felt herself move toward him, slowly, as though she were wading through water. Kat stopped just as her quaking knees brushed against his. He straightened and uncrossed his legs as she approached him.

"I've wanted to do this ever since I walked into that conference room and saw you for the first time," Sam muttered, as his mouth crashed into hers.

It was a frontal attack more than it was a kiss. His firm lips plundered her mouth, his teeth nipping at her lips. She gasped as his hands reached into her hair, loosening the flaming mass from the ribbon that held it. Sam's tongue slid between her lips, sweeping along her tongue, beginning the dance.

Kat's hands were resting on his shoulders, for balance. She felt the heat and sinewy strength of him. He pulled her between his legs, pressing his erection against her belly, as his hands left her hair to cup her bottom.

Sam kissed her with such ferocity that he stole her breath away, insinuating himself into her mouth. His hands began to roam freely over her body. When his fingers pinched her nipples, she squealed in pain and pleasure. He tore his mouth away from hers, his dark eyes searching her face, looking for some indication of resistance. Finding none, Sam stood suddenly, and turned her around. Now she was facing his desk. He came up behind her, his hands firmly grasping her hips. Then Kat felt his teeth nipping at her neck, her ear, the side of her jaw, as his cock pressed against her soft bottom.

She felt suspended there, unable to move, unless he moved her; her senses were so overwhelmed.

It was as if he could not to get enough of her. Sam was pulling up her dress, caressing her thighs, squeezing her round ass. Pleasure tremors moved through Kat, She could feel a warm wetness pooling in her, dripping onto the fingers that were now rubbing at her blue lace-covered crotch. Then Sam was pushing aside the flimsy fabric and plunging his fingers into her.

He pushed her down on the desk, one hand tangled in her hair, the other pulling her damp panties down around her ankles.

"I hope you like it hard and rough, Kat, because that is how I want to take you. Tell me to stop now or that is how it is going to be."

Kat's thoughts were racing as fast as her pulse. She could only form one thought: don't stop. He was in control and she was reveling in it. "Let go," her mind whispered. "Let go and just feel."

She could hear his harsh breathing, like a racehorse in the gate, waiting to be unleashed. Kat turned her face, slightly, so she could see him. He brushed a few tendrils of hair from her face. She smiled at him and simply said, "Yes."

Sam leaned over her until his full length pressed against her. His tongue swirled in her ear. "I'm going to fuck you until you scream, kitten."

He straightened, and she heard more than felt him loosen his belt buckle and undo his pants. The sound of tearing foil came next. Then Sam pulled her hands back behind her. He held them there at her waist. She felt him step in closer to her ass. Her position left her totally open to him. She was starting to tremble from anticipation, from unease. Then his hard throbbing cock was pushing against her ass. His knees were between her legs, nudging them further apart, as she struggled to balance on her high heels.

In seconds, the head of his cock was against her wet nether lips; she could feel Sam's fingers spreading her, readying her for the assault on her senses in the battle she had already lost.

Kat thought he would slam into her, but he slid his sheathed cock in slowly, so slowly she was melting with need.

"Please," she heard herself whisper. "Please. Now."

"No. You'll take it slow and deep."

She was trembling with desire, her cunt was trying to draw him in, but he held her hands down on her back as he moved imperceptibly further and further into her welcoming heat.

He was huge. She felt stretched to the limit, and still he was moving into her. Her mind was screaming it was too much, but her vagina was opening for him. He stopped. Kat's inner muscles were clenching around him, she wanted to move her hips but she was pinned.

Sam's hand was on the nape of her neck stroking the sweaty skin, his fingers dancing in the damp curls. She relaxed for a moment as he massaged her jaw, her neck. Then his cock was slowly sliding out of her. She whimpered in protest, and his fingers slid into her mouth. Kat could taste herself, salty and slick on his fingers.

Then he slammed into her. She screamed. His cock was thick and long and as hard as a lance. Sam pounded into her, holding her firmly in place, silencing her screams with his fingers. Almost all the way out of her throbbing pussy, then all the way in. Long, deep, rapid strokes as she clutched at him, the inner muscles of her vagina the only purchase she had on him, the only hold she could maintain.

The waves of pleasure were mounting. Never had an orgasm built so strongly in her. God, she needed to come, she wanted to come. Kat clenched around him, giving herself up to the sensation of being filled and overpowered, of being taken.

She exploded. Trying to push back against him, his still-strong hold on her kept her in place, but her inner muscles worked him as wave after wave of release tore through her. Over and over again, she could not stop. Just as the tremors were lessening, just as she was coming back to herself, Sam let himself go. The staccato beat of his release, the force of it, pushed her over the edge again, as she milked every drop from him.

The air in the office was thick with heat and the humid smell of sex. Sam was gulping in deep, rasping breaths, still pressed against her. Kat lay across the desk, only his hand on her back keeping her from slipping to the floor in a vanquished heap.

"Are you all right?"

Her lips barely moved, "Mmm hmm."

Sam chuckled. Slowly, he eased himself from her, his hands holding her hips gently in place. "Can you stay still? Don't move. I'm right here."

Kat could not have lifted herself from her prone position if the fire alarm had sounded. She heard the sound of water running. Within a few moments, she felt a warm wet cloth bathing her crotch and her thighs. Then a soft towel drying her. Sam pulled her panties up her legs and straightened her dress.

"Here, kitten, I've got you." He gently lifted her from the gleaming mahogany surface and turned her to face him. Her lips felt hot and swollen, damp tendrils of hair stuck to her flushed cheek.

Stunned, Kat tried to take in what had just transpired between them. But she didn't pull back as he gently wiped her face and neck with a clean washcloth and dried her.

She smiled tentatively when Sam brushed the hair from her face.

"I never did that before," she whispered and a blush stained her cheeks as she realized that she had always wanted to.

"Never had sex on a desk before? Really?" Sam moved to the bathroom to deposit the washcloth and towel. On his way back to her, he picked up her ribbon from the floor and handed it to her.

"Never had sex on a desk." Her voice dropped to a whisper. "And never had anyone...restrain me...like that." Kat was pulling her hair back into some semblance of a ponytail when he spoke.

"Do you want to do that again?" Sam was standing in front of her, looking like he had just walked out of a courtroom—except for his swollen lips and his eyes dark with dangerous promises.

"Now?" She almost squeaked. She was not sure she could walk after being pounded into orgasmic submission on his desk.

"Well, I'm good, but I am not quite that good." He laughed.

"Are you always like that, you know, a little rough and demanding"

"Yes. I like to be in control. Since it seemed that you are pretty much in control too, I knew I would have to restrain you to keep you where I wanted you." He reached out to take her wrists in his hands, rubbing them with his thumbs as if to rub away his harsh grip from before.

His gray eyes met hers with honest directness. "I'll never hurt you. I'll never do anything you don't want, but I'll be the one who decides where and when and how. Can you accept those terms?"

Could she? She wanted him again; the sex had been mind-numbing. Every thought centered in her crotch the entire time. She wanted that release from thinking, from deciding, again. She gave him an almost shy smile.

"Yes, I believe I can."

"Do you want to?" He let go of her wrists. She almost reached for him.

"Yes." Kat paused. "Yes, I want you. I want that amazing cock." Sam laughed at that.

Kat was somewhat taken aback at the boldness of her statement. She added, in an almost shy whisper, "And I need it, for now. For right now. I need the sex, and I need to let go of control." It cost her to say that to him.

His emerald eyes searched her face, as if assessing the depth of her need and the extent to which she could live up to the terms of the agreement he was offering. Apparently satisfied with what he saw, he smiled his lawyer's smile.

"Shall we shake on it, counselor?" His green eyes twinkled as he held out his hand. She smiled as she slid her much smaller hand into his. He gripped it hard. Her eyes widened at the domination she felt there.

"And, just so we understand each other, Kat, while you're with me, you're with no one else. Agreed?"

"You drive a hard bargain, counselor, but yes, I agree." But, when Sam started to let go of her hand, she tightened her own grip. "And I assume that the same holds true for you. No other women for the duration." Now, Kat was smiling her lawyer's smile.

Sam's eyes narrowed a bit, almost as if he were rethinking the deal he had just proposed. But, he shook her hand again and laughingly said, "Of course, counselor. I wouldn't have it any other way."

They left the office together, looking for all the world like two lawyers on opposing sides who had just come to terms over a case. Sam held her car door for her, commenting that he liked that she drove a safe vehicle. With a promise that he would be speaking with her soon, Sam closed her door and watched her pull out of the parking lot and head back to her office.

Much later that evening, after having been secluded in her office for hours with a messy appellate brief, Kat gratefully let herself into her loft condo on Third Street in Troy. She loved the view of the Hudson River from the floor-to-ceiling windows. Dropping her bag on the sofa, she strode to the wall of glass. Looking out at the lights along the riverfront, Kat thought of all that had transpired during the day. She had a lover, of sorts. Someone to have sex with, someone to assume control. It felt like the right choice, like a decision whose time had come but still, she felt a faint guilty wrench twisting in her heart, wondering what Zack would think of all this.

Would he care?

Hugging herself tightly, as though Sam's arms were still wrapped around her, Kat smiled her Cheshire cat smile. Yes, her curiosity about Mr. Robbins had been overwhelmingly satisfied that day. But she still wanted more.

CHAPTER TWO

A few days later, Kat was talking herself out of ever meeting with Sam again. *What am I thinking?* Mia had advised caution, reporting her sources had told her Sam had been playing the field since his divorce the year before. Zack had definitely not been pleased about her announcement that she was seeing a man, and he had given her the third degree. They had been having drinks at Gaffney's after work as they so often did. For what seemed like the hundredth time, she replayed in her mind the conversation they had had the night before.

Two glasses of wine and Kat had found herself telling Zack about a man she had met.

He erupted in a barrage of questions. "Why, after almost ten years of a nun's existence, have you decided to hop into bed with this guy? Who is he? Is he a lawyer? Do I know him? Where did you meet him?"

Kat explained the man was an attorney in Albany and she had met him while handling a case. When the case concluded, one thing led to another and she wanted to see him again.

Never tell a former prosecutor about "some man," she ruefully reminded herself as she took a long sip of her Beune Blanc.

"See him or *see him*? Is my little ice queen finally beginning to thaw? Or did he push you?"

At that question, Kat had blushed furiously. She could still feel Sam's hands on her, pressing her into the surface of his desk.

"No, he didn't push me. I just decided it was time to get back into the game. I was horny, okay?"

"Why now? And why with him?"

Did Zack sound jealous? No, that couldn't be. Zack had been Michael's best friend; he's never showed any interest that way in me. He was probably just concerned about me, as he had always been.

But Zack was eying her suspiciously, as though he could not believe her story.

"I'm almost 40, Zack. Don't you think it's about time? And, he was interested in me. No one has been interested in me *that way* since Michael."

That shut him up. She would swear Zack's turbulent gray eyes had almost twinkled. He backed off then. It was almost as though her statement amused him. He kissed her on the forehead in that big brother way he had, and admonished her to be careful. And then he left, humming some inane tune.

The ringing of her office phone jarred Kat out of her reverie. She expected to hear Cecilia's voice telling her she was leaving for the day.

"Meet me at the Desmond at five o'clock this afternoon," Sam's sexy voice commanded Kat.

"Counselor, good to hear from you. Is this about the traffic ticket? I thought that case was concluded?" Kat bristled a little at Sam's orders.

"The case is concluded, *counselor*. But our business together is not. Meet me in the bar at the Desmond at five." There was a pause, but before Kat could retort she never left the office before six o'clock, Sam's voice dropped to a seductive whisper. "And leave your panties in your purse." He hung up.

It did not occur to her until she was in her car at the ungodly hour of quarter to five in the afternoon to refuse him. To tell him she couldn't leave the office that early. Especially when he knew the hours lawyers, even partners, usually kept. To demand he meet her at a time and place of her choosing.

Like he would listen to me, Kat snorted at the futility of her thoughts. And smiled. She had felt delightfully naughty to not be the last attorney out of the office. In the ladies' room, she felt sinfully liberated when she slid her panties down her legs and tucked them into her purse. And releasing her hair from the chignon at the back of her neck, to shake the auburn masses loose, was heaven. Kat's fingers had trembled as she applied hot pink gloss to lips she had been chewing on since Sam's phone call.

Katarina could feel the heat from the leather car seats burning through the thin layer of her sleeveless linen dress and the body-hugging bra slip she had donned that morning. Feeling freer than she could remember, she rolled down her window to let the breeze from the highway ruffle her already tousled hair. Kat toyed with the top button of her black dress and giggled as she unbuttoned one, then two, of the fuchsia buttons that marched from neckline to mid-calf.

Cranking up the radio, she sang along to "You and Tequila Make Me Crazy." *I am going to order a margarita tonight and see who is going to boss who around.*

The tree-lined entrance to The Desmond cast cool shadows on the brick walkway. The last time she had been there was for a Bar Association meeting. Kat couldn't remember the last time she had gone on a date. *Ten years at least.*

She didn't count the movies and baseball games with Zack as dates. He treated her as a damaged little sister, always kind and considerate, helpful and dependable. For some reason, that irritated her now. Kat knew Zack dated regularly, almost every flight attendant, account executive, model, entrepreneur and recently divorced socialite in the area. Never lawyers. Never widows. And never anyone even remotely appropriate as a future wife.

Not my problem. She straightened her shoulders. She had a date and it was tonight with Hottie Control Lawyer.

Sam was in the pub, seated on one of the Colonial style sofas near the fireplace. Kat's heart pounded as she took the sight of him in. Always so dapper, so confident. His hair sleek, his tan perfect, the pink dress shirt crisp and tailored to his lean body; those long, muscled legs— clad in khaki today— and his jacket tossed over the back of the sofa. Gold watch and cufflinks softly glowed in the dim light; he exuded success. He stood as soon as she approached him.

Kat dropped her pink tote and cardigan on the sofa, next to his jacket. She glanced down at the coffee table where two gin and tonics sat, the glasses beaded with condensation. Tossing her auburn mane, she looked up at him. Sam just smiled as he took her elbow and led her gently down into the chair next to him.

"I wanted a margarita tonight." She almost snapped at him, irritated at the charge she felt when he touched her arm, annoyed at the wetness that was already growing between her legs.

"Not tonight. Tonight is a gin and tonic night. It's July and we're at the Desmond. They make excellent gin and tonics. You want margaritas, next time we'll go to Garcia's."

"You seem pretty certain there will be a next time, counselor."

"We both know there will be more than one next time, Kat." Sam raised his glass to her. "Stop fighting me and enjoy your drink. You look a trifle...overheated."

"I said you could be in charge of the sex. I didn't say you could be in charge of everything." But, she took a long sip of the icy, potent drink. It *was* perfect. *Damn.*

"If I am in charge of the sex, as you so charmingly phrase it, I have to be in charge of the details leading up to the sex." Sam chuckled. "I love how you refer to our intimate relationship as 'the sex'."

Kat had to laugh. He was so sure of himself, so cool and in control. And so sexy. Kat had striven for that kind of control her whole life. But, she came from a messy, loud, Russian Jewish immigrant family of deli owners, grocers and farmers.

She was curvy, hot-tempered, curly-haired, uncoordinated, too bright, too honest, too, too, much. *Different.*

She had learned control to change herself into the woman she wanted to be, the lawyer she dreamed of being, the wife Michael deserved. Kat had attained every goal through sheer force of will only to lose Michael to the capricious winds of war.

"What are you thinking about, Kat?" Sam's smooth voice interrupted her thoughts.

"I'm thinking that you look like the fathers of my WASPY classmates at Emma Willard when I started ninth grade there: all conservative, classy, and cool."

"My sisters and I attended Albany Academy. So do my children. I thought Emma was more...eclectic."

"It is. But there were still those girls who looked like they lived in the pages of *Town and Country*."

"You weren't one of them, I would imagine. All that fiery hair and that smart mouth. I'll bet you drove the instructors crazy." Sam's eyes fixed on her fingers as she stroked them up and down the side of the icy glass. His eyes narrowed as she raised the gin and tonic to her lips and took another sip. After she set the glass back on the table, she let her cold, damp fingers trail down her neck to the opening of her dress, to cool away the heat of the day and the heat from his stare. As her fingers reached her cleavage, Sam shifted noticeably, crossing and uncrossing his long legs, as if he could not get comfortable.

"I've always been mouthy and bossy, comes from my Russian *bubbe*." Kat noticed that he was staring at her mouth again, so she licked her lips, just to see him react. His slightly strangled sigh did not disappoint her.

"Well, I do love that mouth, Kat, and we know who is boss here, so there should be no problems." Sam sipped his drink and smiled.

"Why are you the boss?"

Sam put his drink down. Kat could almost feel the chill that seemed to sweep over him.

"Because I can be. Because I want to be. I need to be in control."

Never patient, nonetheless Kat waited, knowing there was more. His need for control far exceeded hers and she was one of the most controlling people she knew.

"I was raised a certain way: to be like my father, my grandfather, my uncles. Intelligent, athletic, hard working, devout and respectful. I wanted to be a painter, can you imagine?" Sam laughed, a short humorless sound that immediately evoked sympathy from Kat. Her family had never subjected her to a pre-planned life; she was free to choose her own path, as long as she stayed close to family and was a good girl.

Sam's voice softened a bit as he continued. "I always liked to draw and paint. But, the men in our family are lawyers. It never occurred to me to deviate from the path that was set for me. The Academy, Siena College, Albany Law School, the firm. I even married the same type of woman my father and my grandfather had married."

Kat had seen pictures of his ex-wife. Aristocratic, blond, slim, tan and toned in her tennis dress at some fund-raiser at the Albany Country Club. They must have been the perfect couple.

"What happened?" Kat leaned toward Sam, laid her hand on his wrist. Again, the electric jolt from just touching him, that skittered from the tips of her fingers, up her arm and directly to her nipples. She darted a glance down at her chest and smiled at the noticeable reaction to his touch. Sam smiled, too, but the smile did not reach his eyes. He took her hand from his arm, giving it an almost gentle squeeze before he spoke.

"We had three sons. My boys are great. I was happy. I am a good father, I like being a dad—I do. I would have been happy with the three boys, but Connie wanted a girl. So, we kept trying. We lost a baby early in her next pregnancy. Then, we got lucky and in another year, our daughter was born. She is a beauty. Sweetest girl in the world. Three months after we brought her home from the hospital, Connie moved everything of mine out of our bedroom and into a room at the other end of the house."

He swallowed another big gulp of his drink and motioned to the bartender to bring two more over. He looked like a lost boy, and Kat's heart melted a bit at his pain.

The drinks materialized almost instantly. Sam cradled the glass in his hand, staring at the clear liquid as if an answer was floating there with the ice cubes and lime. His voice was hard.

"She was done with sex. She had put up with it to get her daughter and to give me my sons. Now, she was done, she said, with all that messy business and I should be too. I didn't believe her and tried for too long to change her mind."

Kat didn't know what to say. She had always loved sex with Michael. They had mutually agreed to let children wait for a few years while they got their careers started. Then it was too late. But the desire was always there.

"Your family must have been really upset when you got divorced, being good Catholics and all."

Sam's abrupt laugh was bitter. "Being friends with the Bishop has its advantages. We also got an annulment. That eased things a little because you are right—they were not pleased by the divorce. No one in the family had ever been divorced. But, I told my father that the divorce was going through or I was leaving the firm and moving away. He would rather have me around, though disgraced, than absent from Sunday family dinners."

Kat couldn't imagine estrangement from her family. They made her crazy but only because she loved them so much. She spoke to her parents and her grandmother every day and Friday night dinners were often the high point of her week.

Her sympathy must have been plain on her face because Sam stood suddenly and reached for her hand.

"Grab your drink, darlin'. We'll take them to the dining room with us."

Dinner was nice, Kat realized with some surprise. She had always loved The Desmond and its bar, but she really appreciated the quiet elegance of its fancy restaurant, Scrimshaw. Pleasant small talk accented the delicious food. Sam was a great date, she thought. And it had been a long time since she had just relaxed in the company of an attractive man. *Maybe this could work*. She sighed as the tension of the last few days left her.

Sam slid a room key toward her after he asked for the check.

"I'll meet you in a few minutes. The room is off the atrium."

Tension was back, with a healthy dose of anticipation.

Flustered at the thought of having sex with Sam, Kat simply picked up the key and made her way through the lobby. *Please, God, don't let me run into any lawyers I know.*

She had barely put her bag down and turned on the lamp on the nightstand when the door to the room opened swiftly. Sam stepped in, closing the door quietly behind him.

In three strides, he was across the room. Kat had no time to gasp as his strong arms enfolded her and his lips crashed down on hers.

She wrapped her arms around his lean waist, as much to feel him as to keep from toppling over from his amorous assault. Sam's tongue breached her lips and swept through her mouth, dancing with her tongue. He tilted her head back into his hands that had burrowed into her hair and held her there, suspended, while he drank from her like a hummingbird sucking nectar from a bloom. Kat stood motionless in his grasp, unable to move, unable to do anything except absorb the desperation of his kiss. Her nerve endings were humming, her nipples tightened like diamonds and she felt a hot wetness seep from her body. She sagged against him, as though his kisses had sapped the strength from her. *God, he is too much.*

Sam broke the kiss. He straightened, grasping her shoulders to hold her up. He stared into her eyes, as if searching for something. Kat swayed into him, desperately seeking the connection he had broken. Sam stepped away from her.

"Take it off."

"What?"

"Take off your dress. Slowly."

Somewhat taken aback by the curt command, Kat's shaking fingers reached for the fuchsia button at her cleavage, then stopped. *Two could play this game.* Smiling seductively, she bent and unbuttoned the last button. Her hands steadied as she undid button after button, revealing calves, then nothing but the long black slide of her slip. As she unfastened the last button between her breasts, she shrugged her shoulders and the dress pooled at her feet, which were still wrapped in the black leather straps of her high heels, from toes to ankles.

Sam's eyes took in her lush body, clad only in silky black that hugged every curve. "Magnificent," he whispered. At that moment, Kat indeed felt damn sexy.

Sam stepped up to her and slid the spaghetti straps off both shoulders, letting the lacy edge of the slip catch on her deep rose nipples. It hung there as he reached down and grasped the hem of the slip, pulling it up in both hands, his fingers grazing thigh and hip and belly.

Her eyes were huge and never left his face. She stood still, letting him caress her.

"Where are your panties, counselor?"

"In my purse, counselor."

"Good girl."

His fingers played with her nipples, which tightened more and more as he flicked them through the thin silk.

"Can you help me with my tie?"

OUT OF CONTROL: KAT'S STORY

Kat reached around his arms and loosened the tie, pulling it through the stiff collar stays and letting it drop on the floor. She reached for the button at his collar.

"No. I didn't say to unbutton my shirt. You aren't very good at following instructions. You can undo my belt now."

She started to say something but bit her lip instead. Kat kept her eyes downcast, startled by the rapid swelling of his erection beneath the thin fabric of his pants. Her fingers were steadier with the belt, but they strayed against the bulge beneath the fly of his trousers before she dropped the belt to the floor. He was rock hard.

"Shoes and socks, please." His voice was thick with restrained desire.

Kat shot Sam another fulminating look. *Seriously?* But she had agreed to his rules, and she was so turned on she thought she might come at any minute. As gracefully as she could in impossibly high heels, Kat sank to her knees and untied his shoes.

Her posture gave Sam a view of her smooth white back, brushed by her fiery mane. His voice was harsh as he told her to remove each shoe and sock and then stand.

Back on her feet, Kat was pouting. She tossed her head and stared at him, through narrowed eyes. Her hands were on her hips, canted at an angle to him, as if she was deciding whether she would stay or go. One breast was exposed, and Sam reached out and softly stroked it. Then his hand grasped her breast and squeezed, his thumb pressing into her nipple. A wave of pleasure shot from her breast to her vagina and her eyes widened as a needy sigh escaped her lips.

"Now the shirt, then the pants, kitten." Sam's voice was calm and measured. His hand dropped from her breast. He stood straight but relaxed before her, as though he had all the time in the world. The only indication that passion was building in him was his narrowed eyes and careful breaths as he waited for Kat to comply. Kat acquiesced quickly, unbuttoning Sam's shirt, unfastening his trousers. She let her hands caress his chest and shoulder as she reached up to push the shirt off him. He was well-muscled and smooth, tan all over. His trousers hung on his narrow hips. Kat stepped up to him, her nipples barely brushing his chest as she reached behind him to push his pants down. Her hands caressed his tight ass as the pants dropped to the floor.

"Enough," Sam whispered as he turned her, his hands firmly holding her arms. He crossed them over her breasts and his mouth nipped at her neck.

"Nicely done, kitten."

Reveling in the feel of his mouth on her, Kat leaned back against him, his hard length pressed against her. They stood for just a moment. Then, still holding her arms, Sam pushed her away from him. Her slip fell to the floor. She stepped out of it as he began walking her to the bed. Pushing her onto the satiny comforter with firm but gentle hands, Sam stretched her out face down across the width of the bed. She heard his boxers fall away and the thump of condom packs on the nightstand's marble surface. Ripples of anticipation ran down her back. She had to look at him, had to see if his desire matched her own. But his firm hand came down on the nape of her neck. His touch was like a brand, marking her as his own.

"Don't move."

She lay motionless. His hands were like fire stroking her from feet to shoulders, caressing her neck, trailing along her spine, dipping between her thighs. Every time she even thought of moving, of rising into his embrace, of turning to watch him and touch him, his hands stopped stroking and pressed her into the bed. Pleasure quaked in her, little jolts of passion firing in her nipples and her crotch, mounting desire leaving her gasping for breath.

Kat heard the foil wrapper tear open. Seconds later, Sam pulled her up on her hands and knees until her buttocks firmly pressed against his erection. He ran his cock along the crease of her ass, from the base of her spine to her warm, wet curls. Cool air tickled her flaming clitoris as she opened wider for him. The stroking began again except now his hands were running over her breasts, pinching and twisting her nipples at each pass. Those hands possessed her, flowing down to her hips, up between her thighs, across her belly and back to her breasts, teasing her nipples.

Kat couldn't speak. Her senses focused on one thing and one thing only: when was Sam going to slide into her?

His assault was not slow and easy like the first time. If Sam had not been gripping her hips with both hands, the force of him slamming into her would have flattened her. But he held her in position as his throbbing cock battered her with long, deep strokes. All Kat felt was stretching, sliding, withdrawing, sliding in further, until he was almost battering against her womb. But she wanted more. Trying to push back against him was impossible; he had her held firmly in place, so he controlled her movements, the depth of his penetration. But, she arched her back, tilting her pelvis just so.

"Fuck!" The expletive exploded from Sam's lips as he buried himself to the hilt in Kat's scorching, dripping pussy. Kat's gasp was raw and needy and she arched again, like a cat seeking pleasure. It was all either of them needed. Her head dropped to her hands, titling her ass up even further. The orgasm vibrated through her, clasping his length as tightly as his hands were gripping her hips. Sam exploded within her grasp, grinding himself against her, pulling her all the way up so his arms were wrapped around her torso as he pulsed and pulsed, drained of every drop of passion.

They collapsed on the bed, Sam still deep within Kat. He rolled them to the side and just held her as they both sucked in air like runners at the finish line of a marathon.

Kat lay supine in Sam's arms, her breathing finally calming, her skin glistening in the pale lamplight. Then she laughed.

"I have never been fucked like that before. Never. God, you almost killed me. And neither of us are criminal lawyers. One of us would be in the morgue and the other in jail if we hadn't come when we did."

Sam tensed at her words.

"Jesus, did I hurt you?" He turned her over to stare down into her flushed face.

Kat moaned as his movement separated him from her. His face became even more concerned as his hands began running over her. "Did I hurt you? Where does it hurt?"

"Everywhere!" She laughed again, and then seeing the worry in his eyes, she stopped.

Reaching up to stroke his cheek, she whispered, "You didn't hurt me. Shhh, you didn't hurt me. It was just...so intense...so fast and furious. It was...amazing."

Sam stopped stroking, his hand moving to grab her heart-shaped face in one hand. He stared at her as if he were seeing her for the first time. His head bowed down to hers, foreheads touching. "I'll never hurt you. I swear to God I will never hurt you."

"I know that. I do. But, I think..." She paused and her cheeks reddened even more. "I think I like it a little rough. I like it, when you...when you take me. It's not a rape fantasy or anything crazy, more like you are the big strong man and I am the little helpless woman. I...it...well, it turned me on." *Shit, I can't believe I just told him that, and now he is staring at me like I am insane.*

It was Sam's turn to laugh. "Kitten, you are something." He kissed the tip of her nose. "You know I like it rough. I'm glad to hear that you realize that you do, too. And you were pretty good at following my orders." A long tan finger tapped her forehead gently. "But, you don't like being obedient."

"I don't like it. But, I like the sex." She grimaced when she heard him laugh at that. "I mean, the sex is amazing. And, I am mostly okay with letting you run that. I'm just not used to anyone, well, anyone except my grandmother, telling me what to do."

OUT OF CONTROL: KAT'S STORY

Kat sighed, running her fingers through her hair. Looking away from Sam and then looking back at him, her stormy violet eyes finally met his cool emerald stare. "I'm tired of always being the boss. You can be the boss in the bedroom, okay?"

"Okay, and sometimes out of it, too." His right eyebrow quirked, waiting for her response.

"We can try that. But, I know why I want to give up some control, and it's not just for the sex; why do you have to be in control?"

"Because I have been unable to control very little in my life. I let my wife call the shots in the bedroom and look what it got me. It has to be my way now, or it doesn't work for me. It's time for someone else to dance to my tune, and I find I like calling the shots. It's not like I'm going to tie you up or spank you." At the sound of that, a little quiver of desire tingled along Kat's nerve endings. Maybe she could give up a bit more control.

"Deal?" He whispered into her ear.

"Deal."

"Good." Sam's hands clasped her wrists as he pulled her hands over her head, just before his lips sank slowly onto hers.

CHAPTER THREE

"Katarina, what is wrong with you, my *ketzele*?"

It was Sunday morning and Kat was perched on a stool in her grandmother's kitchen, her bare toes wrapped around the bottom rung of the stool, her slim fingers wrapped around the silver-encased glass of hot tea that was placed before her on the worn butcher-block counter.

"Nothing is wrong, Bubbe. What makes you think something is wrong?"

"Because I know my girl,"

"I'm not a girl any longer, I'm almost 40."

"You will always be a girl to me, *ketzi*. Always I remember you as a girl, even when I see the woman you have become sitting right in front of me, chewing that bottom lip, playing with your hair and stirring that glass of tea with such force you are going to break my mother's treasure."

Kat put the silver spoon down and sat up straight. She could never put anything over on her grandmother. Esther Freid Galchinsky had escaped from Russia in 1939, racing from the Nazis and their Cossack henchmen with her family across Europe—to Canada and then New York—by using her wits. At 85, she was as slim and straight as she had been as a girl. Her eyesight had faded a bit and her hands gnarled from arthritis, but she had not lost one brain cell.

And they were all working just fine.

"You think I can tell whether a pitch is a ball or a strike even with my poor eyesight and I can't tell when something is bothering my Katarina? I'm old but I'm not *that* old." Katarina's grandmother attributed her long life and good health to her faith in God, the love of her late husband, a shot of vodka once a day and religiously following the Yankees from the moment she landed in New York at the age of ten.

She sat next to Kat, put a cube of sugar between her teeth and noisily sipped her tea. The glasses and their silver holders had belonged to her mother, as had the bent sliver tongs resting in the sugar bowl—the only valuables that had escaped Mother Russia with her family. "So, what has you sighing and staring into space on this beautiful morning? Have a piece of babka and tell me everything that is wrong." Her wrinkled hand squeezed Kat's smooth one. "You know I will fix it if I can."

Kat squeezed her bubbe's hand right back. Her grandmother had always been her champion. Standing up for her when Kat had been the only girl in a house of boys, and especially when Kat was widowed too young—as her grandmother had been before her.

"Nothing is wrong. It is just that some things are changing and I am not sure I want them to." Kat scrunched her shoulders under her loose white T-shirt.

"Things with the family? What don't I know? Is your brother in trouble with the traffic cops again?" Esther always assumed the boys in the family would cause difficulties, and they often did.

"No, Bubbe, Nate is behaving himself. He can't really speed in a minivan with the babies in the back." Her brother had traded in his sporty Corvette when his wife became pregnant with twins. Now he drove, quite sedately for him, the requisite suburban minivan. That was not to say he didn't tear around in the pick-up truck that was used at the family farm.

"Then what? It can't be your job. You are there all the time, what more could they expect you to do?" Her grandmother had been lecturing Kat for years about her long hours at the law firm, never accepting Kat's explanation that 100-hour weeks were necessary for an associate to make partner, for a partner to make senior partner.

"It must be a man." Esther pointed her arthritic index finger at her blushing granddaughter.

Kat had to laugh. To her grandmother, there were three cornerstones in life: religion, family, love. If all was right with that trinity, then everything else could be managed. Kat shrugged again and looked away, but her fingers fiddled nervously with the frayed edge of her ancient jeans shorts.

"I knew it! I knew you would finally wake up from this trance you have been in for so long. You and Zack have finally gotten together!"

"Zack? No, not Zack." *Where had that come from?* Kat knew Esther had always had soft spot in her heart for Zack—because he was a nice Jewish boy, a boy who always praised her cooking while he danced her around her kitchen after the family meals, to which he was often invited.

"If not Zack, then who? What is wrong with Zack?"

"Nothing is wrong with Zack. I love Zack, just not *that* way." Kat was appalled her grandmother had voiced the notion she and Zack had or could have anything going on!

Kat's grandmother was silent, looking appraisingly at her granddaughter. Kat stared back at her, trying to read the older woman's mind. Her grandmother was always full of questions about Zack and, now as Kat thought of it, always seemed to be pushing them together.

Calm, faded blue eyes met defiant violet ones. Kat would never win a battle of wills with her grandmother. She looked away first. As though satisfied by her triumph, Kat's grandmother smiled. It was a kind smile, but Kat knew what was coming next. She braced herself for her grandmother's version of the Spanish Inquisition. "So, who, then? Who is this man that has you frowning on a sunny day, who has put circles under your eyes?"

"No one you know…and, no, he's not Jewish." Kat answered the question before it could be asked. "He is a lawyer I met while handling a case. He is very nice, but we have only been out once, so don't start assuming anything."

"Who assumes? I only ask, I don't assume. He has a name?"

"His name is Sam."

"So, you are making time with Sam the lawyer? When do I get to meet him?" *God, she is such a Jewish grandmother.* Kat groaned as she answered.

"It's not like that, Bubbe. It's not serious; you don't have to meet him."

"This is the first man who you have shown an interest in since Michael—may he rest in peace—died and it's not serious? Do I look like I was born yesterday?"

Kat ducked her head, letting her heavy curls hide her face. Her grandmother's knobby fingers pushed back her hair.

"So, maybe you are just kicking the tires and taking him out for a test drive, like buying a used car?"

Laughter bubbled up in Katarina. There was no fooling her grandmother about anything. But the image of Sam as a used car was too amusing for her to ignore. She laughed out loud, till tears were in her eyes.

Esther laughed too. Kat could feel the happiness emanating from her bubbe, hear the relieved laughter raucously combining with her own. Kat knew it had been hard on her grandmother, watching her go through the motions of life; no sparkle in her eye, no blush creeping across her cheeks since her husband had died. Kat wiped the tears of laughter from her eyes.

"A used car he's not, Bubbe! More like a brand new Mercedes."

"He's a bachelor?" Kat's grandmother sounded suspicious.

"No, he's divorced. And he has kids."

Esther frowned slightly at this complication and then said, "So?"

Katarina never failed to be amazed at how much her grandmother could put into that one small word. That one word encompassed a world of unsaid yet clearly understood questions: *How long as he been divorced? Who was at fault? Who has custody of the kids? How many kids? How much child support? How much do you know about this man? When did you find out he was divorced, before or after you went out with him? And what makes him think he is good enough for my granddaughter?*

"So, I met him. We went out for dinner once. I like him. He is very smart and very handsome. I went out with him, is that a crime?" Kat responded defensively.

"No, I'd say it's more like a miracle." Esther retorted. Kat's mouth dropped open in surprise.

"You always said not to let people pressure me into dating or getting married again. You said it was perfectly fine if I wanted to stay a widow, to honor Michael's memory." The two women had had many conversations over the years about the loss of a beloved husband, about how people assumed they knew how a young widow felt, assumed they knew what was best for her, and believed they had a right to decide when grieving must end and life must begin again.

"I know and it is…was…fine. But, it is also fine if you want to find someone, if you don't want to be alone any longer. Michael would not want you to stop living just because he did." Esther reached out to stroke Kat's hair, giving it a gentle tug.

"You didn't remarry after Zayde died." Kat had been only a girl when her beloved grandfather had passed away from cancer.

"I didn't, no. But, I was much older than you. I had more years with my husband. And I had my children and grandchildren. I didn't need to marry anyone. You should know that there were times I did not want to go on, but my family gave me a reason to live."

"You were only 55. That's young enough to still be interested in men."

"Who says I wasn't interested in men?" Esther retorted. And now, it was her turn to blush, just a little.

OUT OF CONTROL: KAT'S STORY

"What do you mean? You dated after Zayde died?" Eyes wide, Kat looked at her grandmother in a whole new light. Esther shrugged again, smoothing the skirt of her housedress, her blush deepening, as she looked away.

"Well, let's just say, I wasn't playing Mah Jongg *every* Monday and Thursday night."

"Bubbe! Did Daddy know?" This had definitely not been a subject of conversation around the Friday night dinner table.

"I don't know if he did, I don't know if he didn't. Mothers and sons don't talk about such things. But, let me tell you, I know that a woman has needs. She can deny them her whole life if she wants, but they are there just the same. And if a woman behaves with some discretion, with honesty—so— she shouldn't get those needs taken care of by a nice Jewish accountant or doctor?"

"Who? You have to tell me who. Someone from our synagogue? Someone in the neighborhood? Who?" *Oh my God*, please don't let it be her old pediatrician or the nice old guy who had been doing the books for the family business.

"That is not for you to know. Both of my gentlemen are not with us any longer, may they rest in peace. But, I tell you, your grandfather would have been happy that there was a nice man around to hold my hand, take me dancing at Brown's Hotel, make me feel special again. Not like with your Zayde, but still special."

"So," Esther stood, picking up the now empty glasses of tea and placing them in the sink, "you have a nice time with your gentleman. Be discreet, be honest and don't forget Michael. Just don't think about him *all* the time anymore. It's time to move on. But, you've decided that already. Just be careful, *ketzele*."

Feeling better and worse at the same time, Kat stood and wrapped her arms around the older woman. Guilty she had let her grandmother think there might be any future with Sam.

Happy her bubbe understood and approved of her need to live again, the ache in Kat's heart eased. Kat felt as though her heart, which had not beaten for another for too long, was finally finding a new rhythm.

Now, what the hell had Bubbe meant about Zack?

Katarina pondered that question all day. She left her grandmother's house with a week's worth of clean laundry, chicken soup, and the remains of a chocolate babka. Looking forward to that type of quiet Sunday where you putz around the house, straightening up, changing the sheets, reading the Sunday *Times* and getting ready for the work week, Kat spent most of her time thinking about her grandmother, the doctor *and* the accountant, Sam and Zack. And Zack, some more. She was getting a little annoyed by all the time Zack was spending in her head. So when she saw his number pop up on her cellphone, she answered with some irritation.

"What?"

"*What?* Is that any way to greet your most favorite guy in the whole world? Or have I been demoted to number two by the Mystery Hottie Lawyer?" He sounded so amused. Kat hated it when Zack got that entertained tone in his voice, especially when it was directed at her.

"I'm busy."

"On a Sunday afternoon, you're too busy to talk? What, didn't Bubbe feed you and do your laundry for you today? Tell me you are lugging baskets of clothes up and down three flights to the laundry room at your condo while roasting a chicken, and I'll be right over to help."

"You know entirely too much about my laundry, Zack." Now, she had become amused. It was difficult to be annoyed with Zack for too long.

"I just stopped by your grandmother's house on my way home from the gym. She said you had just left and that she had sent the entire chocolate babka home with you. I had to settle for Linzer tarts."

"Linzer tarts? She didn't tell me she had Linzer tarts."

"She doesn't tell you everything. Apparently, just like *you* don't tell *her* everything." He sounded so smug.

"What are you talking about?"

"Well, over cookies and tea, I got questioned about the Mystery Hottie Lawyer. I swear to God, Kat, your bubbe could have been a stellar District Attorney. I felt like I was being cross-examined." He chuckled and then continued, "Why the hell did you tell her you were dating someone?"

Her irritation faded. "Damn. She wriggled it out of me. I'm like an open book with her. Sorry you had to bear the brunt of this."

"Not to worry, I've been dodging prosecutors for most of my career." He paused, and Kat could swear he was munching on cookies.

"Did she give you Linzer tarts?"

"Yes, she did, because she loves me like a son. 'Here, *tatala*, take some Linzer tarts home so you should have some energy after all your hard work to stay so skinny. I don't trust skinny men, you need to have a little for me to hold on to when I give you a hug,' she says to me. So, I got a dozen cookies and some chicken soup."

"She's feeding half of Troy with that chicken soup. She's going to put Pop's deli out of business if she keeps giving away all that food."

"Not to worry, I stopped by there, too, after I left Bubbe's. Your dad and your brother seemed clueless about the mystery hottie as well."

When Kat started to sputter, Zack cut in "Don't worry, I didn't say anything to them. I just figured if they knew about him, they would be grilling me, too. But all they wanted to talk about was baseball." Kat was sure he had munched through at least three more cookies from the sounds he was making in her ear. But, before she could chide him, he continued. "Hey, that's why I called...well, that and busting on you. Nate gave me two tickets for the Valley Cats' game tonight. You wanna go?"

Two hours later, Kat found herself sitting next to Zack at the ball game, just like she had done a hundred times before. This was the Zack she knew and loved. Scrunched over a hot dog and a beer, his Yankees cap on backwards, unshaven for the weekend, dressed in a ratty Giants T-shirt and shorts, he was her go-to guy, just like always. Kat looped her hand around his elbow and pulled him in for a side hug.

"What was that for?" His soft gray eyes flickered with interest as he looked down at her hand resting on his arm and then back at her face.

"I love you." Her face turned away from him as the crowd booed another strikeout for the Cats.

Kat was grinning when she looked back at him, the inning now over.

"Yeah, I love you, too." He said it the way he always did, like a goddamned big brother or old family friend.

"No, I mean it. Don't be such a guy," she retorted, hitting him in the arm she had just squeezed. "You're always there for me. You and Mia are my best friends in the world. But, she has Steve and the girls. And she hates baseball. What would I do without you?"

"I'm not going anywhere."

"You really should find someone, Zack. You're not getting any younger. You don't want to be pushing a baby carriage at our 25th law school reunion."

"What about you? Think how cute you'll look, pregnant at fifty."

"It's different for me, I was already married. You are going to have to settle down sometime. You'll have no time for me. Then, who will take me to ball games and Bar Association dinners and law school reunions?"

"I will. If I ever get married, I'll marry a non-lawyer who hates baseball."

Kat snorted at that and punched him in the arm again. He never took her seriously when she talked to him about his love life.

OUT OF CONTROL: KAT'S STORY

"So, how's it going with Mystery Hottie Lawyer?" He winked broadly as he said it.

"Stop calling him that." The man was like a dog with a bone.

"Well, you won't tell me his name so what else should I call him?"

Annoyed and uncomfortable with the questions, she snapped, "Just don't call him anything."

"Okay. Then, so how's your love life?"

There were times Kat hated being a redhead. She blushed when she was nervous, embarrassed, angry, drunk. And lying.

"I don't have a love life. And if I did, I wouldn't be discussing it here, or with you." Kat, huffily retorted, and turned her attention back to the game.

Zack drilled a finger into her side. "Why not? I tell you about the models, the flight attendants and the real estate agents."

"Yeah. So, how's *your* love life, then?"

"I gotta tell you, I'm now putting real estate agents on my no-date list. They're never available on weekends, and every one of them wants me to sell my condo and buy a house in the country. In East fucking Greenbush, for God's sake!"

Snickering with him, at the thought of cosmopolitan Zack living in the country, with a lawn tractor and a snowplow, far away from all his favorite delivery joints and his gym, was too much.

"No lawyers and now, no real estate agents. You're going to be running out of dating prospects very soon, *tatala*. You'll have to lower your age limit."

"No way. They can't be young enough to be my daughter, even if we lived in the wilds of Washington County. No one under 30. I'm actually thinking of moving it up to 32. That will eliminate interns and residents who are too busy to date anyway, and junior executives and associate professors. I think I might try some psychologists next."

Kat laughed so hard she almost spit beer on the lady in front of her. Zack dating a shrink? What fun that doctor would have with him and his inability to commit. But, she sobered at the thought; he *was* pretty committed to her. Just no other woman, except maybe Bubbe. Zack's mom had died recently of breast cancer, and he was an only child. Now that his dad had moved to Florida, Kat's family had practically become Zack's family.

"The lawyer and I had a date on Thursday night." *Where had that come from?*

"Really? Where did you go—a lecture at the law school or a porn film at the Third Avenue Theatre?"

"Stop." She hit his arm again. "We had drinks and dinner at The Desmond."

"Did he spring for a room or did you just neck in the back seat of his car?" It was said laughingly, but there was a tightening around Zack's mouth as he darted a glance over at Kat.

Her face was flaming now, even in the cool breeze that had come up as the sun was setting. She hugged herself, as though chilled. Zack put his arm around her, rubbing her shoulder as if to warm her. Kat turned into him and whispered into his ear, "He got a room."

Zack's fingers dug into her shoulder but his voice remained calm, almost disinterested.

"Was he any good?"

"What kind of a question is that?" Kat demanded.

His eyes on the game, he replied, "Well, I'm thinking it's the first time in almost ten years that you've gotten any, and I was hoping he'd be good enough to have made it worth the wait."

There was a long pause, before Kat whispered in his ear again. "It was worth the wait."

That answered his question. But her answer left so much unsaid. She'd had several orgasms, so yeah, the sex was good.

It was great. But, Kat was still a little concerned about Sam's control issues.

"It was good, but different," she continued. "I mean, it wasn't like Michael, but it was good, it was really good. Except...." There was something bothering her and she really wanted Zack's take on Sam.

"Except what?" Zack was staring at her now and he seemed almost angry. And a little worried.

She didn't want him to think that Sam had hurt her. Quick to assure him, she whispered, "Nothing bad. But...I can't believe I am telling you this...but he doesn't like to do it facing me. He likes to be, you know, behind me." Kat ducked her head behind the fall of red hair that was fairly sparkling in the harsh glare of the stadium's night-lights.

Zack's voice was gruff and low. He leaned over, his eyes still on the debacle that the ninth inning had become and, *sotto voce*, asked, "Doggie style?"

"Yeah, sometimes, or variations on that."

"Sounds to me like he has control issues."

"How did you know that?"

"Because he doesn't want to look in your face and be distracted. And he certainly isn't going to let you be on top."

"I cannot believe I am having this conversation with you."

"Who else are you going to have it with? Mia, your secretary, your mom? I'm it, Kat. I'm the only person you know who you can talk to about anything to do with sex." Zack laughed and tugged her up out of her seat. The game was over, the Valley Cats had lost again and it was time to go home.

He walked to her door, like always, waited till it was unlocked and she was inside. But when she turned to hug him good night, he bent and brushed a kiss on her cheek. Before Kat could say a word, Zack turned and silently walked away.

CHAPTER FOUR

By the end of August, Kat figured she had experienced more orgasms at Sam's hands, and other body parts, than she had experienced alone during almost ten years of widowhood. And the workouts he put her through were better than any class at the Y. Her body felt loose and limber, and even the old guys at work had commented on her easy, gliding walk.

Face it, girlfriend, she told herself one morning as she was climbing out of her car at work, after a late night with Sam, *the sex*, as they both were calling it now, *was fan-fucking-tasic!* Sam still insisted on calling the shots, still controlled every aspect of their intimate encounters, still preferred fucking her from behind. But it was great, wasn't it? She had not felt so well used since the early years of her relationship with Michael when they were law students, fitting sex into their crazy lives as often as they could.

And their dates were fun. And interesting. Just never anywhere his family or hers, or their colleagues, might run into them. At least they had agreed on that. Sam didn't need any complications with his ex-wife and children, and Kat certainly did not want to be fielding questions from her family, friends and partners. They only went to dinner locally in their business suits after work, and would have appeared to be two lawyers discussing a case over drinks and a bite to eat. Weekends found them heading out of the area, to New York City or Lake Placid or Stockbridge, for concerts, museum visits and hours of sex in country inns and nondescript chain motels.

And she liked him. Kat really liked him. He was interesting. He was courteous and kind. He was damn good-looking. That and *the sex*, she snickered to herself as she gathered her things and headed up to her office, was enough. Way more than she had since Michael died. And she still had Zack.

The ringing of her phone interrupted her reverie later that afternoon.

"Counselor." Sam's voice brought a smile to her tired face even though it was the end of the day and there was an evil headache brewing behind Kat's eyes after long hours of reading an appeals record that had to be at least a foot thick. "You didn't respond to my e-mail."

"I've been buried in a case file almost all day. I haven't looked at my computer since I walked in here this morning. What did your e-mail say?"

"I reserved seats for us at the Bar Association's New York Practice Update in Saratoga on Friday morning. I wanted to make sure you put it on your calendar."

"I wasn't planning on attending; I have so much work to do on this brief."

"I want you there. We'll do the Bar luncheon at the Track after and then we can spend some time in Saratoga."

"You want to hang out at the Track and then traipse around a town full of lawyers, most of whom we know or who know one of us? What happened to discreet?"

Sam chuckled, that "master-slave" chuckle he had sometimes when she questioned him.

"I don't think it will be a problem. There will be so many lawyers around that we will just blend in."

"Blend in? My hair is like a fire alarm, and you are all tall and commanding. We don't blend in anywhere." But he insisted, so after the call, Kat sent an instant message to Cecilia to pencil in the Bar Association on Friday. Her secretary popped her head into the office seconds later.

"I didn't make that reservation."

"I know. I did."

Cecilia's eyes widened in surprise.

"Why? You don't need any more continuing legal education credits this reporting period."

"I wanted to hear Professor Spiegel speak on the topic. It's New York Practice." Kat's voice sounded defensive even to herself.

"You think Professor Siegel is a conceited jerk, you have since law school." Cecilia was like a private eye sometimes; she would not let anything go.

"Well, I'm mellowing, Ceci. Just put it on my damn calendar, will you?" The headache was pounding in her skull, and Kat was nearing the end of her patience.

Cecilia drew herself up to her impressive five-foot, five-inch height, stiffened her spine as only a pissed-off secretary can, and almost snarled, "Yes, ma'am. Do you want just the morning blocked out or the whole day?"

"The whole day."

This was too much even for Ceci. Sarcasm dripping from her voice, she retorted, "A whole day to attend a half-day class on a subject you know everything about, for credits you don't need, taught by someone you can't stand. So…what's the deal?"

They had known each other too long. Kat had hired Cecilia as her first secretary, and they had been together ever since, through their marriages, through Michael's death and Ceci's divorce, through Kat's journey from a cubbyhole on the second floor to a corner office on the fourth, through Ceci raising her daughter on her own.

"It's a date. I have a date on Friday." It was time to be honest with Ceci.

Of, course Ceci didn't believe her. "Right. You don't want to tell me what's going on, fine. But don't give me a bullshit answer like you have a date to take a CLE course. You, dating? A lawyer? Give me some credit." Cecilia turned toward the door in a huff. Then she paused and turned back. "Unless it's Zack. Is it Zack?"

"No, it's not Zack. Why would it be Zack? Why does everyone think I should be dating Zack?"

"Because you want to date Zack, but you're afraid to do it."

"I'm not afraid of Zack."

"No, but you're afraid of falling in love with Zack. Zack is the real deal. And you can't boss Zack around." They stood glaring at each other. But then, as if seeing something in Kat's face that answered all her questions, Ceci just shrugged and said, "But, hey, you want to go on a date to the CLE class in Saratoga with some mystery lawyer, far be it from me to stop you. Consider it on your calendar, boss." And with that, Cecilia flounced out the door, letting it close a little too loudly behind her.

Why does everyone in my life seem to think I am with Zack, should be with Zack, or even want to be with Zack? Can't they see that he doesn't think of me that way? And, of course, I don't think of him that way either. Rubbing her head to try to ease the now full-blown headache, Kat was faced with an almost equally horrifying thought. *My, God, what if I need reading glasses?*

Friday was one of those gorgeous mid-August days in upstate New York. The sun was warm and the breeze was gentle. A few fluffy clouds dotted the azure skies and the trees along the Avenue of Pines were dark green and lush, their bases surrounded by generous mounds of white, pink and red fuchsias. The Gideon Putnam, at the edge of the Avenue, stood in stately grace, its brick façade faded by the decades past, the striped awning rippling crisply in the breeze.

Kat pulled her bright red car into the lot, parking just a few spaces away from Sam's gleaming black Mercedes. She laughed to herself. Y*eah, that's Sam—all dark, solid and expensive. And this is me,* she thought as she slammed the door on her Volvo. *Flashy on the outside, but inside, reliable and sturdy.*

Sam was at the long table outside the conference center, filling a cup with coffee from a glistening silver urn. *God, he is gorgeous.* Tall, dark and handsome. Lean and impeccably dressed in business casual, khaki trousers crisply pressed, yellow Lacoste polo shirt under a navy blazer, shiny cordovan loafers on his narrow feet. She nodded to some former classmates gathered near the door and headed to the refreshment table.

"Counselor." His deep voice hid a hint of humor in the otherwise innocuous greeting.

"Why, its Sam Robbins isn't it? It's been a long time since.... What was our last case together? Oh, that little traffic incident, wasn't it?" She smiled brightly, that fake smile one lawyer gives to another, that smile that says, "Yeah, and I can beat you again, sucker." Sam's eyes swept over her, head to toe. Business casual for Kat never meant slacks. She usually avoided pants; she didn't think she had to dress like a man to be respected. Her navy print skirt flowed from her curvy hips to her slim ankles, the soft aqua cotton jewel-neck sweater, picking up one of the colors from her skirt. Her navy flats matched the small navy bag hanging from her shoulder and the navy bow at the end of her French braid. She looked sexy and carefree.

Passing a tea bag to her, Sam leaned in and whispered seductively in her ear, "Are you wearing panties?"

Kat could feel the blush on her cheek. "Of course, I am." Her voice dropped to a husky whisper. "Why do you ask?"

"Take them off then come sit next to me. Hurry along, kitten. The lecture starts in five minutes."

She wanted to stick her tongue out at him, but there were too many lawyers around. A few minutes later, Kat slid into the seat on Sam's right. At the sight of his raised eyebrow, she licked her lips and nodded affirmatively. His nostrils flared, she noticed with some satisfaction, and she was sure the shifting he was doing in his chair was not just because the seat was hard.

She stifled a giggle and opened the folder in front of her.

OUT OF CONTROL: KAT'S STORY

Two and a half hours of Practice Updates later and Kat was again wondering why she had let Sam bully her into wasting her morning. Until they stood, and she felt his hand on the small of her back. He was guiding her to the garden doors opening onto the parking lot.

"Why don't we take my car to the Track? No sense in both of us jockeying for parking spots." He laughed at his own play on words.

"You want to drive over together? What about keeping all this to ourselves?"

"We're just two colleagues sharing a car. What are you worried about?"

They were at their cars. Kat unlocked hers to toss the folder of class material on the seat and retrieve her wide-brimmed navy straw hat from the seat. Twining her long braid up around her head, she slipped the hat over the coil, anchoring it in place with a flowered hatpin. Sam whistled long and low over her transformation from casual to sophisticated.

"Baby, you should wear your hair up all the time, shows off that sexy neck of yours." He helped her into his car and closed the door. Sliding in on his side, he leaned over and planted a kiss on her neck before he started the car.

Where had this publicly possessive and demonstrative man come from? They had been careful up to now, but Sam was acting like a lover. In public. It was the same all afternoon. From the special parking lot the State Police waved him into, through the VIP gates and up to the Clubhouse, he was right next to her. His hand on her elbow, his hand at her waist, his hand brushing her shoulder as he seated her at their table overlooking the finish line, Sam was constantly finding reasons to touch her. And every time he did, Kat melted a little more. She was acutely aware she was not wearing panties, especially when the errant breeze threatened to lift her skirt as they took the escalator down from the Clubhouse at the end of the sixth race. Every caress had set sparks off in her, so that by four in the afternoon, she was edgy, needy and wet.

And her clit was throbbing.

In the car, Sam reached over as they drove back down Broadway to the Gideon Putnam and slid his hand under her skirt to the top of her thigh. Touching her wet pussy lightly, he brought his fingers back to his lips, sucking the tips, all while wearing a naughty grin.

"I am about to pass out over here, in case you hadn't noticed."

"I noticed. I'm as hard as a rock." Sam pulled her hand over to his crotch, pushing it down on his throbbing erection. "We're almost there."

"Where? The parking lot? I am not having sex with you in your car in the Gideon's parking lot. I don't care how hard you are or how wet I am." Kat had to draw the line somewhere, because Sam seemed to be throwing all caution to the wind.

"I got a room."

"When?"

"I reserved it when I registered for the update. I picked up the key this morning. We can go right up. Five more minutes, ten at the most, and I'll make you come."

She groaned, the pulsing between her legs increasing tenfold at his promise.

As good as his word, Sam had her in the room in five minutes. The lock clicked in place, Kat pressed against the door with Sam behind her. His strong hands swept up her legs, around her hips and into her crotch in one seamless movement. One hand spread her nether lips to flick at her clit while the other hand was busily inserting one, then two, fingers into her throbbing heat. The orgasm rocked through her. She bucked hard against him, but he gave her no room to move. Then Sam's hard length pushed against her bottom, as he held her hips in place. His lips were nipping at her ear as Kat gave herself over to the waves of sensation.

OUT OF CONTROL: KAT'S STORY

The last spasms of the orgasm were still rippling through Kat, when Sam pulled away from her. She started to turn, but he kept her pressed against the door. She heard his zipper and the tearing of the condom's wrap. Seconds later, he entered her slick channel. He slid all the way into her in one long, hard thrust. Several more deep thrusts and he came, his hands in a death grip on her hips, his breath burned her neck.

When he was done, they stood still, Kat plastered against the door, Sam plastered against Kat.

"You okay?" Sam's words muffled as his lips moved in her hair.

"I don't think my legs are working," she laughed. "I feel like a train ran over me."

Strong arms lifted her and swung her into the room. Kat's breath left her lungs. Shock swept through her. No one had carried her since Michael had carried her across the threshold on their honeymoon. It felt the same. And different. Michael had been as tall as Sam. Years of swimming had given Michael a wide chest and muscular arms and back. He had been brawnier than Sam, but that feeling of weightlessness was the same. That feeling of being in the arms of the chivalrous knight was the same. Feeling protected and cherished. But, this was no knight in shining armor; this was Sam. Her lover, her sometimes controlling, always demanding lover.

As if she were insubstantial, Sam carried her across the room and laid her gently on the huge four-poster bed. She felt as if she floated in the clouds, sheer white drapes above her, fluffy white comforter enveloped her. Sighing, she looked at this man. A bemused look played over Sam's face, as if he were seeing her for the first time. A small niggling worry crept into her head. *What was going on here?* Sam had been openly attentive all day, in public. So far, no demands from Sam, except lose the panties at the conference that morning. *Now, he is behaving like the lead in a romantic movie.*

She sat up and stared at him. Sam smiled and turned away toward the bathroom. Within moments, he emerged, shrugging off his sports jacket, kicking off his loafers. His shirt and trousers followed in short order. Clad only in his boxers, he approached the bed, tossing the foil packs in his hand on the nightstand. Then he reached out to clasp her hands, and pulled her to her feet.

"Your turn." Sam sprawled across the bed. "Make it slow and sexy, kitten."

Easy enough. Kat's gaze locked on Sam's emerald eyes as she kicked off her flats. Gripping her sweater at the hem, she pulled in increments up her torso and over her head, dropping it on the chair he had used. Her fingers never fumbled on the clasp between her breasts, her aqua silk bra falling open to reveal breasts tipped by hard rose nipples. Watching Sam watch her turned her on all over again. Kat slipped the skirt down over her hips and let it drop in a soft puddle at her feet. Stepping out of the skirt, she raised her hands to undo her braid.

"Leave it." Sam softly ordered. "Come here." He sat up and slid to the edge of the bed, his legs spread, his cock already swollen and erect.

Kat sauntered across the spacious room and stopped in front of him, her knees touching the bed. Maybe this time they would make love looking at each other. Sam's long fingers reached out and pinched her swollen nipples. Pain and pleasure shot right to her dripping pussy. Then his mouth was on her, sucking her nipples, licking them as he kneaded her breasts, moving from one to the other, until her knees started to buckle. She swayed and he caught her.

"Stand still, kitten, don't move." He reached over to the nightstand for a condom. In seconds he was fully sheathed. *Now*, she thought, *now we will make love, face to face.*

Sam kissed her. His tongue was magic in her mouth, teasing her, devouring her. Then, he turned her in his arms, nipping at the nape of her neck, running his tongue down her spine. One hand pulled her back, onto his hard length. His other hand twisted her braid, pulling her head back.

He slid his cock into her, one hand buried in her wet curls, stroking her throbbing clit as he eased all the way into her. Sam immobilized Kat with his tight hold on her braid, his hand buried between her legs, and his cock impaling her. His teeth sank into her shoulder as he thrust, short, hard pulses, into her. His thumb pressed on the hard nub of her arousal with each thrust. Her ass slapped against his thighs as Sam fucked her hard, fast and without a sound, like a stallion mounting a mare.

She came. Hard. With no way to move, and only her inner muscles, grabbing hold of his cock, squeezing him, the orgasm seemed to sweep into her very core, climbing up, up, her body until she was shaking and sobbing. "Please, please, please," burst from her lips. Tears erupted from her eyes. And still he kept up the short, hard thrusts until she collapsed against him. Then Sam came, on a long moan that tore his mouth from her shoulder.

Moments later, he eased her back onto the bed. Totally spent, she curled into herself. Kat felt the bed move as Sam rose. She heard the sound of water running in the bathroom. She did not move, did not speak. As always, Sam washed her clean of their passion. He sank down behind her, pulling her back against him, his arms wrapped around her.

"God, I think you killed me." Her voice was a satisfied whisper.

He chuckled. "If I did, we're both dead because I think I saw heaven." He kissed her neck. "Damn, Kat, sometimes I just can't seem to get enough of you."

"Well, I think I had all of you and more tonight, Sam." She paused. "But, what was that all about?"

"What do you mean?"

"Today. All the touchy-feely stuff. Tonight. This room. All of it."

"Kat, I've been thinking." She froze in his arms. "I'd like us to move forward." *Move forward? What the hell does he mean by that?* "I think we should start being more open about our relationship. I'd like you to meet my family."

At that, Kat broke from Sam's embrace and turned to face him.

"Relationship? Meet your family? Your kids? Your parents? Where did that come from?"

"Well, we suit each other. We've been seeing each other for several weeks. There's no one else…is there?" Sam's eyes searched her face.

"No, we made that clear at the start. Exclusivity. But, that's not what you're asking me, is it?"

"I think we make a great couple. We should move forward."

"There it is again. Forward to what? We're lovers, nothing more." At the frown he threw her way, she added, "We like each other so we're friends, too. And we share the lawyer stuff."

"Like I said, we're good together. We make a good couple."

"Sam, what is this really about? Are you trying to tell me that you've fallen for me?" Kat could not believe that was what he meant; maybe he was trying to get her to join his law firm, because his reasoning just sounded way too much like a business deal being laid out for her.

"No. I'm not in love with you, but I do care about you." Sam looked away and then back at Kat. She was still staring at him, but now her eyes scrutinized him. Kat was trying to read him—his words, his voice, his actions, in the same way she tried to read an opponent in any legal transaction.

"Look, here's the deal. My father is retiring as County Court Judge at the end of August. Only a few people know. I've been approached to run to fill out his term. It's rather short notice, and the other side will have to scramble for an acceptable candidate." Kat was still staring at him, but realization was beginning to dawn in her eyes.

OUT OF CONTROL: KAT'S STORY

"So, Sam, you have to clean up your act. No more divorced guy playing the field. You can have a lady-friend, but she has to be respectable, age appropriate, no baggage. And it probably doesn't hurt that I am a war widow and Jewish. That would hit two target groups: Jews and veterans. It works." Kat felt dread in the pit of her stomach. She liked Sam, she really did. And she would have been happy to continue their love affair for a little longer because the sex was mind-blowing. "So, do you just want me draped on your arm until Election Day or is this to be a long-term arrangement?"

Sam reached out to stroke the damp tendrils away from her face. "Well, my father's term has two more years. Then I would have to run for a new full term. But, we would work well together. Maybe we could make the arrangement permanent."

"Damn, you're sweeping me off my feet here, Sam. A 'permanent arrangement?' That's about the most romantic proposal I've ever gotten."

"Don't be mad, Kat. I do care about you. And the sex..." Sam laughed at that and tugged her braid. "The sex is amazing. It could work."

No, no it could not work. She liked him, but she would never love any man again. She was sure of it. And she would not tarnish the memory of her marriage to Michael with a marriage that was a sham.

"I'm not mad. I'm just sorry that we have to end this now. I can't be in a relationship with you, Sam. I can't marry you. I can't marry anyone. It's not in me. And it's not in me to pretend."

He started to protest, but she silenced him with a kiss. It was over. Kat wouldn't discuss Sam's proposal any further. She dressed slowly, shaking her head as he repeated all of his previous arguments.

"Counselor, you make a good case, but there's no appealing my decision. I can't do it. Even for 'the sex.' And the sex was amazing. Thank you for that. I wish you luck with your campaign. I'd even vote for you if I lived in Albany County. But, we're done."

Without another word, Kat turned and walked out the door. Before he saw her tears. They kept spilling out of her eyes as she drove home in the dwindling light. Why was she crying? She didn't love Sam, she never would. But, he had taught her to feel again. He had made her want, need, the touch of a man, the hard length of a man buried deep within her. And the surrender.

She was back in control again. No more moments of delicious submission. And that loss she regretted most of all. *Submission.*

CHAPTER FIVE

It is too damn hot. It's two weeks past Labor Day, and all of a sudden, it's summer again.
In Buffalo, no less.

Kat scooped her hair off her neck and up into a messy top-do, securing it with a rubber band from her case file. The anemic puffs of cool air from the train's air-conditioning provided some relief as it hit her sweaty neck and shoulders. *That's better.*

The train had been idling at the downtown station, fifteen minutes past its departure time, due to "slow switches" on the track ahead. *I should just have driven.*

"Sorry for the delay, folks, but everything is fixed now. We'll be leaving momentarily." The conductor's voice floated through the car. It was mid-afternoon on a Thursday, and Kat was tired, perspiring and annoyed. It had been years since she had argued an appeal before the Appellate Division, Fourth Department in Buffalo, and she had thought it would be a nice diversion to take the train from Albany to Buffalo and back. Besides, she could get some work done on the train. All had gone according to plan on the trip out. She had even had the opportunity to have dinner the first night with two friends from law school who were practicing in Buffalo.

It was a nice distraction from thoughts of Sam, which still ran through her mind when she was drifting off to sleep. Or waking up. Or just about any time when she was otherwise unoccupied. He had called a few times to get her to change her mind, but she had held firm.

Kat knew she had made the right decision, even Zack agreed with her. Zack. Smug son-of-a-bitch. He had all but said "I told you so" when she informed him she and the Mystery Hottie Lawyer were no longer together. Zack had made some condescending remark about her taste in men and then just grinned at her in an oddly possessive way. Like he was thrilled she was alone again. He had started calling more often, dropped by unannounced a few times. And, frequently, his arm draped across her shoulders, his lips left lingering kisses on her forehead. There were even a few swats on her tush that felt vaguely un-brother-like.

He was behaving very strangely. As the train began to move, she stretched her legs out to the seat across from her. When the train wasn't crowded, she always chose the middle row of the train, where four seats faced each other. She knew it was selfish, but she liked to stretch out and have room next to her too. Her legs were bare, panty hose tucked into her tote bag in the Courthouse ladies' room, along with her black pumps. Black ruffled flip-flop sandals were much cooler and comfortable for the dash to a cab and the long train ride. Her purple linen jacket on the seat next to her, she had undone the top and bottom few buttons of her sleeveless black linen shirtdress. She was finally relaxing as the car cooled down and picked up speed. An iced chai and the latest issue of *Vanity Fair* were going to keep her company for the next few hours.

"Is this seat taken?"

Damn. Kat pulled her feet off the facing seat and looked toward the deep male voice. *Damn.* Smiling down at her were very blue eyes, edged with very curly eyelashes. The rest of him wasn't bad either.

"You don't need to move your feet...you look like you need to stretch out and relax...I just need the one seat." He was stowing a backpack in the overhead rack. The faded denim fabric of his shirt stretched over his muscular shoulders and forearms—lightly dusted with freckles and reddish blonde hair—were revealed under the rolled up cuffs. He sat in the seat diagonally from her, tucking his long khaki-clad legs under the seat next to her. She glanced down. He was wearing cowboy boots. Kat discovered in that moment that she had a thing for cowboy boots.

"No, it's quite all right; I'll just tuck them under." Kat swung her legs down, revealing for an instant a flash of white thigh, before she primly tucked her dress around her.

"Really, I don't mind. It's a treat to look at your pretty silver toes."

Kat blushed. She had forgotten that her weekend trip to the nail salon with her two little nieces had resulted in her letting them choose a new color for her toenails: a glittery gunmetal grey. Her cheeks flushed an even deeper shade of rose when she surreptitiously checked out Sexy-voiced Stranger while he was handing his ticket to the conductor.

His curly reddish-blond hair was a little long and had a little silver threaded through it. His bushy mustache matched, as did the hair she could see curling at the open neck of his denim work shirt. His rugged features were lightly tanned, slightly sunburned, as if he had just returned from a weeklong fishing or camping trip. He wore a narrow silver bangle and a slim dark brown leather bracelet with a silver clasp around one wrist, a beat-up serious-looking watch on his other. No wedding ring, just a braided silver band on the ring finger of his right hand. Damn, he was interesting. And hot.

He tucked his ticket into his breast pocket and focused those piercing blue eyes on Kat.

His hand extended to her, he introduced himself. "Hello, seatmate, I'm Rick Sheridan."

"Katarina...Kat...Galchinsky." Her hand was lost in his large paw, warmed by the heat of his grasp. And there it was again, that little shudder of excitement shooting all the way to her gut. And below. He squeezed her hand briefly, as if he felt something too, and then let it go.

"Where are you headed today, Kat?" His gaze was direct, his voice low and interested.

Kat relaxed a bit. Perhaps she had been imagining that jolt of pleasure.

"Albany. But I live in Troy."

"Me, too. I mean I'm going to Albany, but I live in Cambridge." He explained he lived above an antiques shop on the Main Street of the colonial town and loved being within walking distance of the growing number of restaurants and shops in the refurbished village.

"Did you have business in Buffalo?" *Is he an antiques dealer?* He didn't look like one.

"No, I was working in Toronto and caught a ride with some of the crew down to Buffalo. They're flying back to LA, I'm just heading home."

"What do you do?" They asked at the same time. Laughing, Kat pointed to her briefcase.

"I'm a lawyer. I was arguing an appeal in Buffalo."

"Screenwriter here, though on this project, more of a consultant than a writer."

"What project?" This occupation fit his look, she thought, but he seemed a little self-possessed for a creative-type like a screenwriter.

"An indie film about a veteran coming back from the wars, with a little too much information that certain bad guys would like kept secret."

Kat nodded, a military background would explain his air of command and discipline. She asked, "Are you a veteran?"

"Yes, ma'am. I'm a Marine." Rick straightened a little as he answered. He raised an eyebrow when Kat nodded as though she recognized something about him.

"You guys never say 'I was a Marine' even if you have been out of the service for years." She smiled and then sipped her chai.

"Well, you know, *semper fi* and all that. Once a Marine, always a Marine."

"I know. The Army can be like that, too." A tinge of sadness, and a little regret, squeezed her heart.

"Lots of good men...and women...in the Army." Rick paused and looked at her more closely. "Are you Army?"

"Only by marriage."

Rick glanced down at her left hand and then at her right. Kat had long ago removed her swirled gold wedding band from her left hand and moved it to her right.

"My husband, my late husband, was in the Army JAG."

"I'm sorry for your loss." Rick reached over and took both Kat's hands in his. "Did he die in the service?"

Kat looked away, though she made no move to take her hands from his. Somewhat stiffly, she answered Rick.

"Yes, he died in Iraq ten years ago. An IED blast took him and his driver."

"I'm so sorry. He was a good man." He squeezed her hands and then released them.

Her voice was barely audible. "Yes, he was. The best. But how would you know?"

"A lawyer...you said JAG...in Iraq, ten years ago? He had to have volunteered right after 9/11. Lawyers didn't just get sent to Iraq, not like combat troops and other specialties. No insult intended, but lawyers weren't needed as much there as combat troops were. I'm guessing he volunteered to be sent to Iraq. So, a good man, who saw his duty and served his country when others might not have."

"Yes, that was Michael. A good man." Kat looked away again. She was blinking to hold back the tears. It felt wrong to be discussing Michael with another man, even if he was a veteran, too.

Turning back to him, she asked, "Were you in Iraq?" Maybe that was why she sensed empathy from him; he might have served where Michael had served.

"Yes, I was, on a few missions. Mostly, I was in Afghanistan."

They rode in silence for a while, to the Rochester station. Passengers got off and more got on. Finally, Rick spoke again.

"If you don't mind my saying, you seem awfully young to have been a widow for ten years."

"We married right out of law school. I had just turned 30 when Michael died. He was almost 31." Again, that momentary pang of sorrow.

"I'm sorry if my questions brought up bad memories."

"No, it's all right. I just don't usually discuss it with someone I've just met. I don't know why I did that."

"People say I have a sympathetic face." Rick laughed. "I can't see it; this old face is about as sympathetic as a rock cliff."

"No, no," Kat laughed, feeling better, "it's Robert Redford rugged, all manly and stoic."

"Now, you've made me blush. The red in my hair seems to show up on my face every time a pretty woman gives me a compliment. And it's been a stretch since that happened."

"I bet you have to beat them off with a stick."

"No, I'm lucky at staying alive but unlucky in love." He looked deeply into her eyes. Kat felt an answering blush creep across her cheeks, down her neck, lower. Her nipples hardened at the raw speculation she saw in his eyes.

"Do you still take that many risks?" Kat was toying with the button on her dress, the button that was just above her cleavage, the button that was hiding a glimpse of her lush breasts from Rick's view.

"Well, like I said, once a Marine, always a Marine...." Staring at her fingers, Rick's voice trailed off. He stood abruptly and, with an "I'll be right back," headed down the aisle.

What the hell is happening here? Kat fidgeted nervously in her seat. *What sent him scurrying away?* She stared out the window at the farmland and villages flashing by, glimpses of the meandering Mohawk River revealed through breaks in the dense brush along the tracks.

"Here you go." An icy plastic cup, dripping with condensation, filled with golden beer, was thrust at her.

"Umm, thanks. What's this for?"

"I'm drinking to our first date." He touched his glass to hers. Kat smiled and took a long sip of the cold beer. She had to give him credit for his chutzpah.

"Our first date? Here on the train?" Flirting and a cold beer could count as a first date, she supposed. But, Rick laughed again. He had such an infectious laugh. He tilted her chin with his thumb and forefinger, so she was looking into his beautiful blue eyes.

"Honey, I think I can do better than that. I'm drinking to the date we're going on as soon as I ask you out and you say yes. I didn't think I had a chance when I sat down, but I'm thinking now that there just might be a possibility that you would go out with me."

So, he had recognized the gleam in her eyes as something more than just polite interest.

She turned to glance out the window at the passing landscape then turned back to him.

"Marine, we're coming up on Amsterdam. It will be only 30 minutes after that, and we'll be arriving in Albany. You don't have a lot more time to screw up your courage and ask me." She took another long sip of beer and licked her lips.

Rick's eyes strayed to her mouth. Then he looked her straight in the eye and asked, "You will go out with me. Say yes."

"Yes. Yes, I will." Kat's heart was beating hard within her chest. There was something about this man, his air of command tempered by his sense of humor and polite demeanor. Rick was leaning back in his seat, smiling a decidedly wicked grin.

"Cool." He reached out for her hand and brought it to his lips. They were cold from the beer, but his kiss burned her knuckles as if he was branding her. "You won't regret it."

CHAPTER SIX

She was already regretting it. *I've been picked up by a stranger on a train.* For almost ten years, nothing. And now, in the space of a few months, one lover down and another potential lover knocking at her door. Saturday night and she was going out on a date. With Rick.

They had parted with a handshake at the Albany train station parking lot, after he walked Kat to her Volvo in the parking garage. Moments later, as Kat waited for the light, she watched him walking across to the long-term lot where he climbed into a dusty green Jeep. They had exchanged phone numbers, so she was not really surprised when he called a few hours later to make sure she had gotten home safely. Over the day and half, they had spoken twice: late Friday night for what seemed like hours and early Saturday morning. She learned Rick had been married and divorced, twice. He had one son, married, with one child—the grandson he adored. He lived in Cambridge because he had grown up nearby and there were cousins and an older aunt residing in town. But the true love of his life was a cottage on Long Beach Island, on the Jersey Shore.

Rick was fifty, he told her, almost as an afterthought. He had attended the State University at Albany before he had been selected as an officer candidate in the Marines. Rick had retired from the Marines as a Captain in 2008, but then said nothing more about his service.

There he was, leaning against the doorjamb. Looking like an urban cowboy from the tips of his beat-up cowboy boots, to the crisp white shirt tucked into faded jeans, sleeves rolled back to showcase strong wrists and silver bracelets. His hair was still a bit damp but curled in sexy ripples around his face and the nape of his neck. He was holding a bouquet of sunflowers tied in raffia.

"Yee haw," Kat said with a laugh, standing aside so he could enter her loft. "You look like you should be line-dancing in Austin instead of schlepping around Third Street in Troy."

"So do you. Jeans suit you." Rick bent to plant a warm kiss on her cheek, his arm snaking around her waist for a quick squeeze. Taken aback by his possessive squeeze, Kat stepped out of his embrace and reached for the flowers.

"For me? I love sunflowers."

He seemed nonplussed by her reaction to his hug and smiled as he placed the flowers in her hands saying, "I picked the flowers this morning from the garden behind the shop. I'm glad you like them."

Kat caught him watching her tush as she walked away into the kitchen to find a vase for the bright yellow blooms. She smiled to herself. Her ass looked good in the dark navy jeans she had matched with a low-cut thin cream sweater. She had wrapped her neck in a long, gauzy scarf of autumnal flowers printed on taupe that matched her taupe suede flats. Rick had said Dinosaur Barbeque was their destination for the evening, so she knew jeans would be perfect.

He had turned toward the windows where the lights from the river were just coming up.

She placed the vase on the sofa table and joined him.

"I love the view from here. Makes me feel like I'm in Europe sometimes, living in an old factory on the river."

Once again, he slipped an arm around her waist, but this time she did not move away from him. "I love living near water, too. Not in Cambridge, of course, though the Hudson River is so close. But I live for the shore." He nuzzled her mass of red hair. "You smell good."

She turned her face to his. Their eyes met and held. She could see the river lights reflected in his deep blue eyes just before he bent to kiss her.

Rick's mustache tickled when he gently touched her lips. No pressure, just a soft sweep as if in greeting and then it was over. But, Kat had sensed his restraint and felt the strength of his arm as he had pulled her ever so slightly closer. Her breast was tingling as it brushed against his chest. His kiss and his touch had aroused her immediately, making her achingly aware of how much she wanted him. But, she wasn't sure yet if she wanted to jump right into a sexual relationship.

She stepped away from his embrace and said, "I'm starving. Are you ready to go?" Kat scooped up her bag and met him by the door.

They took the elevator, chatting about the weather and the waning light so early in the evening brought on by autumn's approach. His aged green Jeep Cherokee was parked in front of her building. It was an adventurer's rig, a few mud spatters on the fenders, piles of gear in the back. It took only a few minutes to drive to the restaurant with Kat pointing out areas of the downtown that were undergoing restoration.

Dinner was fun. Rick was fun. They bonded over margaritas, her drink frozen and his on ice. He attacked a full rack of ribs while Kat made a heroic attempt to finish a huge slab of brisket.

"God, I love brisket," she mumbled, wiping spicy sauce from her lips. "I can never finish what I take, though. This is great, but my grandmother makes the *best* brisket. I love family dinners when brisket, which she calls pot roast, is on the menu." Kat watched his midnight eyes follow her fingers as she licked sauce off each one before using the wet wipes.

"I love a woman who eats. And enjoys her food. Too many people starving in the world to waste food the way some do, taking two bites then just pushing food around their plates."

"Well, I'm taking this home with me; it will probably feed me for three days. And whenever I have leftovers, I am a happy girl. I hate to cook." Kat grinned when Rick reached over to wipe a few stray drops of sauce from her chin.

"I love to cook, especially barbeque. I'd be happy to feed you anytime."

After their meal, they sat on the deck, enjoying the cool breeze coming up off the Hudson River, and the lights from the city. Music was playing somewhere. Rick caught her hand in his and bit her palm lightly. Pleasure and pain mixed through her system. Her eyes widened and her breath caught as his tongue licked out to touch the faint indentation his teeth had left.

"I could eat you up, right here, Kat. You are one interesting, beautiful, sexy woman. I'm amazed that you have been alone this long."

"Until recently, I had no interest in dating. I just focused on family and work."

"What changed?"

"I met someone. And I surprised myself by being interested enough to see him for a while."

"What happened? I assume you are not still together."

"He proposed. I said no. That was the end of it."

"He loved you, but you were not in love with him?"

"I liked him very much, he liked me, too, but I don't think he loved me. It was more of a career move for him."

Rick took another sip of his drink and stared at her for several long moments. "Well, I really like you, but I'm not going to propose marriage."

"Good, because I'd have to turn you down if you did."

"I do have some other proposals you might be interested in, though. Would you care to go somewhere private to discuss them?"

Once again, they conversed easily on the short ride from the restaurant. But Rick's thumb kept stroking the palm of Kat's hand, the hand that was resting on his well-muscled thigh. In the elevator, he turned her to him, and wrapped his arms around her, holding her close. She could feel the hardness of his erection and was sure the diamond points her nipples had become were practically piercing his chest.

The door to her apartment had barely closed when he drew her into his embrace. This time the kiss was long, and slow and deep, his mouth totally possessing hers, his hands twisted into her mass of hair. She held onto his waist to anchor her amidst the swirl of sensations buffeting her. *The man can kiss.* And his mustache totally changed the sensations, providing an extra caress that she could definitely get used to.

Rick broke the embrace, taking a step back from her, but still holding onto her arms.

Kat's eyes searched his. *Is he ending just the kiss or is he ending the evening?* Reaching up, he began to untie and unwind her scarf. Never taking his eyes from hers, he slid the length of it from her neck and shoulders. One hand was holding her wrists together. The other hand draped the scarf over her joined wrists. She looked down and then slowly met his gaze again. Rick started wrapping the scarf around her wrists, looping it once, then twice. Both ends trailed almost to the floor, her wrists softly yet securely bound together.

"Do you like a little pain with your pleasure?" Rick asked, his voice a rough whisper.

Kat licked her lips, looked back down at her wrists and felt a jolt of pleasure at the sight of the scarf tying them together, and then whispered, "A little, yes."

"We'll start with a little then." He moved her toward her bedroom, using just the scarf to pull her along. Closing the door, he glanced around the room. Soft light from the lamp on her dresser, which she had left on earlier, bathed the bedroom. A wicked smile crossed his luscious lips as he reached out to pull her bathrobe from the hook on the back of her bedroom door. He tossed it on the bed. Her eyes widened. Rick tied the ends of the scarf in a double knot then nudged her over to the door.

"Raise your arms up, Kat. I'm not going to hurt you."

OUT OF CONTROL: KAT'S STORY

She did as he asked, feeling the familiar tightening in her gut and the seeping of hot desire between her legs. He looped the knotted scarf up over the hook that had held her robe, pulling it tighter so her arms stretched above her, thrusting her breasts out. Rick ran his hands down her arms, lightly caressing her swelling breasts, and then brushing across her belly to her crotch.

"Now, that little hook is not going to hold you fast. One good pull and you'd be loose. But, I don't want you to do that. I want you to leave your arms up. I want you to listen to me and follow my instructions. Can you do that?" When Kat nodded, Rick continued. "If there is anything happening that you don't want, you just have to say a safe word, and I'll stop. Okay?" Kat nodded again.

"What is your safe word?"

Kat didn't have a rational thought in her head, as excited as she was about what was to come. So, she whispered, wryly, "Safety."

Rick laughed and said, "Okay." Then, smiling a wicked, sexy smile, he stepped up to her.

She thought she had been kissed before but she was wrong. Rick was a warrior, and his kiss was an onslaught to her lips, her mouth, her chin, her neck, her brow. His tongue swept into her mouth then was gone, licking a hot trail to her ear, where it swirled, sending shockwaves to her groin, before he dropped hot wet bites along her neck and collarbone. The soft hair of his mustache was a gentle counterpoint to the sharp nips of his teeth. His hands were buried in her hair, massaging her scalp, caressing her shoulders, then holding her face while he rained kisses on her eyelids, nose and cheeks. Always, there was a sharp little bite, soothed over by his soft mustache and then taken into a deep kiss by his clever, clever lips.

Kat was writhing with need. The pull on her wrists seemed to heighten the sensation of every movement as she rubbed herself against him. Then he pulled her sweater up over her breasts. Both his big rough hands squeezed her breasts, pinched her nipples through the thin silk of her bra. She moaned in need, into his mouth as her tongue danced with his.

Rick broke free of her kiss. Watching for her reaction, he freed her breasts from their silky captivity, gathering them into his hands, pressing them together so that his mouth could capture both of her nipples at once. Kat's hips jerked against him when she felt the twin pull on her throbbing peaks. He licked and sucked until she thought she would burst and then he bit, gently, as he held her breasts to his mouth.

Gulping air, Kat was trying not to pull too hard against her restraints. She wanted nothing so much as she wanted to wrap herself around him. Nothing except the intense pleasure she was feeling as Rick plundered her helpless body. Then he stepped back. Kat moaned at the loss of contact.

"Sshhh, baby, just give me a minute to get you out of those sexy jeans." Kat was already kicking off her flats. Rick unfastened the button at her waist, his fingers caressing her belly as he undid the zipper, his hands squeezing her ass when he pulled the jeans down her legs His fingers slid into her silk panties, touching her wet curls for a moment before her bikinis were in a soft heap with her jeans. He knelt to lift her feet from her discarded pants. Blowing a kiss over her swollen nether lips, he nipped her inner thigh. She jerked in response.

Looking up at her, their eyes met. Rick's eyes were wicked and knowing. Still watching her, he swung her right leg over his left shoulder. His fingers parted her, holding her open, then his tongue gently flicked against her clit, and she was lost. Suspended against the door, unable to touch him, she was at his mercy as he devoured her. *The man knows how to kiss. And lick and suck and bite.* Again and again he brought her almost to peak, then eased back with a soft kiss on her pulsating nub before he began again.

"Please, oh please, God, Rick, oh, please." Kat heard a woman's pleading voice and realized it was hers.

"Yes, ma'am." And with a quick nip, he buried his face between her thighs, sucking her as he inserted two fingers into her molten passage. She came on a long, low, almost feral growl, fucking his mouth with rapid jerks.

He stood, smiling that dangerous smile and bent to kiss her. She could taste the salt of her passion on his lips. While she gasped for breath, Rick unhurriedly loosened his belt and pulled off his jeans, grabbing a condom from the back pocket before he kicked the pants out of his way. He unbuttoned his shirt but left it hanging open, Kat saw the mat of honey-blonde hair spread across his chest.

Unwrapping the condom and pulling it down over his impressive cock, Kat could almost feel Rick's eyes on her face. She was looking at his erection, though, licking her lips. Liking what she saw, she smiled.

He stepped into her; nipples bruised by his bites, hardened even more as the crisp chest hair abraded them. His cock was pressing against her belly.

"Do you want me to take you down? Do your arms hurt?"

"My arms are fine, but I want to touch you." Her voice was almost pleading with desire.

Rick shook his head "no" and tapped his finger on her nose, like an adult instructing an errant child. "No touching for you. What else do you want?"

"I want you to fuck me."

He laughed. "That you can have."

He lifted her onto his cock, holding her ass in his hands, opening her to him. He pushed into her in one long smooth glide. Buried in her, he growled, "Wrap your legs around me, sweetheart, and hold on."

It was like nothing she had felt before. Suspended above him, unable to touch him, she was the receiving end of a battering ram. Rick's powerful thrusts pinioned her against the door as his cock hit every nerve ending in her sleek passage. Within moments, she was clutching around him, squeezing him as he pushed into her and then withdrew, only to push in further. His breath was coming in gasps, and then he exploded. His climax brought Kat to her second orgasm, more intense than the first. His head dropped to her shoulder as his breathing slowed.

"Damn." Kat's voice was a ragged whisper in his ear.

"You are amazing. Let me catch my breath, and I'll get you down." Rick mumbled into her neck, nibbling along her shoulder before he planted a noisy wet kiss on her swollen lips. Cradling her bottom in one hand, he lifted her slightly so her bound hands slipped off the robe hook. Wrapping his arm around her, he turned and, still embedded in her, walked to the bed. He laid Kat gently on the soft comforter and eased from the warmth of her body. She lay supine and satisfied. After unbinding her wrists, then pulling her sweater and bra off, he grabbed the throw at the end of the bed and tucked it around her.

Kat was still floating on the high of her two orgasms, her body relaxed and feeling well used. After a quick trip to the bathroom, Rick climbed in behind her.

"I have to say, darlin', that you are game. Have you played at this before?"

"What? Unbelievable sex? Yeah, I've had amazing sex before. There was a pretty long dry spell, but before that it was great."

"No, I mean the bondage part, the you-being-helpless and me-being-in-control part."

"Well, not before. Not with Michael. But, since, well, I've found I like not being in control. And, yes, I want sex to be a little rough."

Turning her into his arms, Rick kissed her softly, sweetly. Kat melted into his embrace. Then he bit down on her lower lip, a quick sharp nip. The sting made her gasp, the shot of desire that arrowed straight to her groin made her grin.

"Yeah, like that. I take it that is how you like it, too? A little pain with your pleasure?" Kat sucked on her throbbing lip, craving more.

"Baby, I'm a giver not a taker in that respect." He brushed the hair from her face, the damp auburn strands that curled riotously on her forehead and cheeks. He gazed into her smoldering violet eyes, as though he looked for something else.

She looked away, unable to take the intensity of his stare.

"You ever wonder why you like it a little rough, a little out of your control now? It was pretty good sex with your husband before he was killed?"

She winced at the harsh word. She always said that Michael had passed away or had died in Iraq. *Kill* was a word she avoided. Rick was gripping her face, forcing her to look at him.

"Yeah, it was like that for me, too. I married my first wife right out of college, right after Basic Training, before I went to Officer's School. We had dated the last two years of school. She knew I was joining the military. I had huge school loans, and what else do you do with a degree in International Politics and Geography? But, as it turned out, I also had an ear for languages. The Marines sent me to a special school in Maryland. I was there for two years learning Mandarin, Korean, Arabic, Hebrew, to go with the French and Spanish I took in high school and college. Life wasn't too bad. My wife, Elizabeth, was a nurse. She was at the National Institute of Health, working on infectious diseases. We were happy. Our love life was great: sweet, satisfying, fun, just not too adventurous because, hey, what did we know?" His voice had dropped to a harsh whisper.

"We were still kids. We had our baby boy before Elizabeth was 25. Right before I got my first deployment. I didn't see him or my wife for over a year. They had to get to know me all over again. Then I was shipped out again. By the time I got back stateside, they were gone. She couldn't take the separations. I gave her the divorce with no arguments. She had not signed up for that gig—raising a kid alone. They were living in California. The only good thing was that my son still wanted to see me, so whenever I got back to the States, I spent whatever time I could with him. He turned out good, a good man. Married a sweet young woman and gave me a grandson last year." Rick smiled a bittersweet smile. "Named him after me, but they call him Ricardo. Best present I ever got."

Sadness swept through Kat. She could feel how lonely his wife must have been, but she could feel his need to serve and his stoic acceptance of what that service had cost him. She brushed a kiss over his lips, wrapped her arms around him and waited for him to continue.

"Anyway, I was traveling all over the world, but mostly in Asia and the Middle East, with a couple of stops in Africa. It was too crazy and too dangerous to get involved for any amount of time with any woman. Till I met Sybill. She was attached to the State Department. Smartest woman I ever met and the toughest. We danced around a little bit, but one night after a few too many drinks, we hit the sheets. There was nothing tender about that woman, not a drop of sweet in her. And it worked." Kat couldn't take her eyes off Rick's face. It had changed, hardened; his eyes were bleak and distant.

"All the sweet and tender had been leached out of me, too, by what I had seen, what I had done. My wife, Elizabeth, she saw it in me, that first time I came back, and it just got worse. It was the same for Sybill. The only way it worked for her was rough. I didn't want anyone who could make me feel what I had felt for Elizabeth; I couldn't let my guard down enough to love like that again. Well, me and Sybby, we got drunk enough on some down time in Vegas to get married. And six weeks later, when we finally sobered up, we got divorced in Mexico. That was it for me."

Kat was watching him intently. She saw the hurt that was still there under his almost nonchalant description of his two marriages. It only made her feel closer to him. She gulped down the emotions that were rising in her, before she confessed to him, "I know what you mean. I can't feel anymore what I felt for Michael. I will never love anyone like that again. And I don't want to. That was for Michael. But, I want to feel."

And she had realized it was the loss of control that gave her the freedom to just feel. She didn't have to think about who she was or what she was doing. She didn't have to worry the sex would be mistaken for anything other than what it was: mutually given and received physical release.

As if reading her thoughts, Rick said, "And, if there is some pain, then the pleasure is okay. It's like you're paying your dues for the pleasure. So, it's not taking anything away from what was your husband's. It's different, it's out of your control and it takes you out of your head. No thinking, just feeling."

When Kat nodded, Rick said, "Yeah, it's like that for me, too. Except I need to control it, I need to dominate it, so there are no mistakes, no chances for a mishap. No one gets hurt." Cocooned together in her soft bed, Rick and Kat did not whisper endearments to each other. Her arms wrapped around him, their legs tangled together, Kat's face cradled in Rick's hands, they shared their pain, their anger and their fears, words tumbling out of mouths bruised by the kisses they also shared. And when they moved together again, still facing each other, Rick tightly held Kat's hands behind her back, her leg draped up and over his hard thigh, as he filled her and fucked her, until she was sobbing his name.

This man, Kat thought, this man did not tend to her in the aftermath of their stormy joining, like she was his prized pet, like Sam had done. This man dressed silently, his eyes never leaving her face. This man, this soldier, patted her bottom and threw her a cocky salute before he turned and left her bedroom. When she heard her front door close, Kat climbed out of bed, wrapped in the comforter and strode to the window that looked down on the street. She saw Rick exit her building. When he got to his Jeep, he paused for a moment. He looked up at her window, smiled, and then shook his head almost in disbelief, before he drove away.

CHAPTER SEVEN

"I've got bagels. You want?" Zack's voice seemed to shout from Kat's cellphone. It had to be just past dawn on Sunday morning. Kat stole a glance at the clock: eight o'clock. *What the hell?*

"What are you doing up so early?"

"What are you talking about? I've already been to the gym. Haven't you already been out for a run? Wait…are you still in bed? Are you sick?"

Kat was not sick but she ached in every joint, a good ache, but she still felt rode hard and put up wet. She stifled a groan.

"I'm not sick. I was just up late last night. I must have forgotten to set my alarm." She had also forgotten to put on a nightgown or brush her teeth, but Zack didn't need to know that.

"I'm coming over. Get up so you can buzz me in. Do you want chai or just green tea?" He actually sounded concerned. But, that was so like Zack.

"Green tea. With lemon."

"You don't need to remind me, I know how you like it." Chuckling, Zack hung up.

Kat smiled to herself and said to the empty room, "He has NO idea how I *like* it, now," before she scrambled out of bed to clean up. Within fifteen minutes, she had brushed her teeth while in the shower, pulled on black leggings and an oversized gray T-shirt, thrown her discarded clothes in the hamper, shoved the comforter and pillow shams into their proper places on the bed and straightened the robe hook on the back of her bedroom door before she re-hung her robe.

When the buzzer from the lobby sounded, she was just taking plates and napkins out of the kitchen cabinets. By the time Zack was knocking on her door, she had the curtains drawn and the Sunday news on the TV. It looked like nothing untoward had happened in her apartment the night before.

"So, who were you out with last night, the Mystery Hottie Lawyer who you have not mentioned in a few weeks, or someone new?" Zack started the interrogation as soon as she opened the door.

"What makes you think I was out with anyone last night?" Kat took the bagel bag and hot cups from him before she closed the door. Stepping up to the kitchen peninsula, she busied herself so she wouldn't have to look at him.

"Duh! You slept in and you're not sick. You've showered on a Sunday morning and you haven't been to the gym. If you were just hanging out for the morning, you would have only brushed your teeth and washed your face...if that. So, you must have been getting rid of the evidence of a night on the town...makeup, etc., or the traces of a heavy-duty romp in the sheets."

He peered through the open door into her bedroom. Turning to her, he laughed a sharp laugh. "Guilty as charged. Romp in the sheets. You never make your bed on weekends."

During the week, Zack looked like he had stepped out of the pages of *GQ*. He wore finely tailored suits, perfectly matched ties, polished shoes and subtle jewelry. Not a hair out of place and neatly shaved—even when running late for court. He dressed like the epitome of the successful, respected lawyer. On the weekends, however, he looked like a slob. Unless he had a date. Zack and Michael had shared the title of "Worst Dressed" all three years in law school.

Michael favored painter's jeans, gray T-shirts, and beat-up Docksiders with no socks except in the dead of winter. Faded blue jeans and old baseball jerseys, teamed with Converse All-Stars that were so dirty they were gray and not white, had been Zack's daily uniform. And they both wore the oldest, rattiest flannel shirts in cold weather paired with Union sweatshirts and the ugliest navy down vests. It was a wonder Kat had even agreed to go out with Michael considering his outfit on the first day of classes.

Still, sometimes Zack's good looks caught her unawares. Like this morning. Sunlight from the loft's windows picked up the gold highlights in Zack's curly brown hair. The two-day stubble accentuated his lean face and the dimple just to the right of his mouth. A faded Yankees T-shirt over worn jeans clung to his muscular frame. *Just like law school.* He looked all athletic and male and very...hot. Kat looked away, the telltale blush staining her cheeks. *When did I start thinking of Zack as hot?*

The bagels were still warm. *He does know me so well.* Sesame with tomatoes and cream cheese for Kat, pumpernickel with olive cream cheese for Zack. They both hated lox; the unusual shared dislike of the smoked salmon had been one of the first facets of their friendship. She plated the bagels, poured her cardboard cup of tea into a heavy red ceramic mug and perched on one of the stools at the counter.

Zack sipped the black coffee from his cardboard cup and stared as Kat took a big bite of her bagel, reveling in that first mouthful of Sunday morning deliciousness. She licked a smear of cream cheese off her lip. Zack shifted in his seat. Kat reached over and squeezed his thigh.

"If I didn't love you already, *tatala*, I would love you forever just for this bagel. Still warm. The *best.*"

"I love you, too, you greedy whore...primarily, because you can be had for the price of a bagel and a schmear. You're too cheap."

"I may be cheap, but I'm not easy." Kat threw back one of their old law school lines. They had all been so broke in law school that an-all-you-can-eat Chinese buffet had been a fancy night out for them. It was still one of Kat's favorite dinner dates—to munch her way through an entire smorgasbord of egg rolls, fried rice, and General Tso's Chicken. Michael had always teased her about being such a cheap date.

"I don't know if that's still true. Who was here last night and when did you meet him?" Zack's tone was not playful now; all trace of teasing had disappeared, as had the easy camaraderie. Kat bristled at his tone and his assumption. She didn't like this Zack who was always questioning her. *Who does he think he is?*

"I picked him up on the train from Buffalo. He's a twice-divorced ex-Marine who drives an ancient Jeep and lives in Washington County. And he's way older than me."

Coffee spurted from Zack's lips at her outrageous statement. Kat smugly sipped her tea as she passed him a few napkins to clean up his mess. Too late, she noticed the bruise running across the inside of her wrist. Turning her arm, she dropped the napkins by Zack's plate. She was not fast enough. He grabbed her hand and flipped it over. A thin red line that was starting to color was readily apparent against her fair skin. Then he took her other arm in his hand. The bruise on the outside of that wrist was already deepening to purple.

"What the fuck have you been up to, Katarina? Playing war games with Captain America?"

"No, we were playing Sultan and harem girl. What do you think?" She snatched her wrists away. Damn him for making her feel uncomfortable.

"So, you've moved from an in-control lover who can't look you in the face to an in-control lover who likes to tie you up. Is that what you're saying?"

"I'm saying that it's none of your damn business who I fuck or how."

Kat could see Zack's temper flare. He looked at her intently for a moment, then closed his eyes and breathed deeply. Regaining his composure, he said, "It is my damn business because I am your friend and I love you. It's my damn business to intervene if you have gotten yourself involved with some man who is abusing you."

OUT OF CONTROL: KAT'S STORY

Kat huffed out an annoyed sigh. He was right. He cared for her. He was just looking out for her. But, it was hard to tell Zack what was going on and that was unusual. He had often been more of a confidante than anyone else, including Mia.

Not so lightly punching him in the arm, their signal that all was going to be okay between them, she said. "I'm not being abused by some man. I don't think I could or would allow that to happen and you know if some man—or anyone—came at me, I'd have the police up their ass as fast I as I could dial 911. We, Rick and I, were playing around and he tied up my wrists. I wasn't supposed to pull on the ties but, you know, one thing led to another..." Her voice trailed off as she saw a red flush creep across Zack's cheeks. *Damn, have I embarrassed Zack?*

"So, you are moving along the BDSM highway, is that what you are telling me?" He kept his voice neutral, but she caught a slight tremor in his hands as he lifted the disposable cup to his lips. And he shifted again in his seat.

"BDSM? Is that what it's called?"

"Jesus, Kat, haven't you heard of *Fifty Shades of Grey*? Every woman I know has read it."

"Yes, I heard of it, I'm not dead. I just didn't pay much attention to it. And they were calling it 'mommy porn'. I'm not a mommy and I don't read porn." She stuck her tongue out at him. "Except maybe *Lady Chatterly's Lover*. I was just curious about getting tied up, so we tried it."

"So, the bondage part was *your* idea?" Kat could see the tension around his mouth and the narrowing of his eyes. He swiveled his stool slightly away from her, but she saw the way his shoulders rose and fell as he obviously tried to control his breathing.

"Well, no, it was his idea. He likes to dominate, like the Hottie Lawyer." She snickered.

"But, he doesn't seem to need to always do it, you know, not facing me. He just likes me to do what he wants the way he wants, if you know what I mean." Now, her cheeks were burning.

Zack shook his head and took one more deep breath before turning to face her. He swallowed once, hard, before he asked, "Are you going to see him again or was this just a one night experiment?"

"I don't know. We just started all this. But, I do kind of like the tied-up part. I would try that again, I think."

Zack wiped a slightly shaking hand across his face. He looked away, his eyes straying from the windows to the couch to Kat's somewhat perplexed face. He took another sip of his coffee and motioned for her to continue.

"So, what's the other part of that BDSM stuff? Bondage, domination, sado-masochism, right? I don't know about the sado-masochism part—is that like whips and beatings and stuff? I'm not sure I would want to do *that*."

Zack almost choked on his coffee. Kat felt a twinge of regret at the direction their conversation had taken, but Zack was her closest friend. The one who had stood by her through the loss of Michael—and the one who was here with her as she reawakened. Zack's expression shifted, almost imperceptibly, to a face she didn't recognize. A face that reflected some inner conflict, some unspoken desire.

Alarm bells went off in her head. Maybe she shouldn't be talking about her sex life with Zack.

CHAPTER EIGHT

It was late on Friday evening and the salt tang of the sea air whipped through the open windows of Rick's Jeep, pulling long curls from Kat's ponytail and sending them flying around her face.

"I love it! I love the ocean. I can't see it yet, but I can hear it and I can smell it. I love this!"

Rick reached over to brush the hair from Kat's face. "I love it too. This is my place, my refuge. Has been for 20 years." He made a left turn from Long Beach Boulevard onto First Street. Within a moment, they were pulling into the driveway of a tall, narrow house.

Kat could see the moonlight reflecting across a long path on the ocean, from horizon to beach. It was like a Winslow Homer painting. She felt a weight lift off her shoulders. Kat had been working so many hours on an appeal she had just argued that the days had run together. And, several evenings with Rick had left her with only a few hours of sleep. Even her worries about Zack's troubling attitude faded away.

Rick made short order of unpacking the Jeep, removing his backpack and Kat's suitcase.

Kat had already scrambled up the steps at the side of the house to the deck. The beach and the Atlantic Ocean spread out before her, deserted on this early October evening. The air was warm, stirred by the cool ocean breezes. She heard Rick behind her as he unlocked the door to the cottage, the thump of their bags hitting the floor. Then his arms were around her, clasping her hands across her chest, as he pulled her back against his hard body. She felt that tug of protection she experienced when in his arms, the feeling Rick controlled her fate and would let nothing hurt her.

"I can see why you love it here. The view alone is worth everything." The house was built on top of the street-level garage so that the first-floor deck and walkway crossed over the top of the sandy dune separating the street from the beach. Its construction provided an unimpeded view of the ocean and private access to the beach.

"I didn't suffer too much damage from Hurricane Sandy, because the garage and a utility room are the ground floor of the building. But I had to replace the deck and walkway, most of the roof, and many of the windows. Some water got in and a lot of sand. I had it better than most of the shore people and I'm handy with tools, so I was able to do much of the work myself that winter. It was a good escape for me, rebuilding and renovating my house and some others down here. Gave me a lot of time to think."

He kissed her hair and then pulled her into the house. She saw immediately Rick's presence was everywhere, and nowhere. The open floor plan's beachy-nautical theme bespoke his love of the ocean and his association with the Navy, but there were no photographs of him, friends, or family anywhere. Paintings, pillows and tchotchkes from around the world adorned the walls, shelves and benches, obviously gathered on his travels, but nothing that any adventurous tourist could not have found in a slightly out-of-the-way souk, marketplace, or port town. White was the predominant color, with bright accents everywhere, and it was immaculately clean. Like Rick, Kat thought, a neutral canvas, with a few splashes of color, randomly placed, with no apparent connection, no easily ascertained meaning.

He took their bags up to the second floor while she inspected the first floor kitchen. A bottle of Riesling was chilling in the fridge; she found wineglasses and a fancy corkscrew on the bar in the dining area.

OUT OF CONTROL: KAT'S STORY

By the time Rick came back down the stairs, she was already on the deck, lounging in an Adirondack chair, her bare feet propped on the railing. From the corner of her eye, she saw him pause in the doorway, taking in the view of the water, before his gaze shifted to her, totally relaxed and sipping wine in the moonlight. Kat's belly clenched, in delicious anticipation of what the weekend would bring.

"It doesn't get any better than this, darlin'." He slid into the chair next to her, gratefully taking the glass she extended to him. "Are you hungry? I had the market on the corner stock the fridge and the cupboards so I've got a little bit of everything to eat."

"Don't move. I'm fine. I'll fix us some cheese and fruit in a few minutes. Let's just relax. And toast to this beautiful evening." Kat tapped her wine glass against his and smiled. "Thank you for bringing me here."

"Thank you for coming." He took a long sip of wine then put his glass down on the deck between them. "I like this skirt," he said, as he eased a hand up the thigh that was revealed when the frisky breeze caught the gauzy fabric and lifted it above her knee.

Kat started to push the bright print back down, but catching the gleam in his eyes, she relaxed and let her legs drop slightly apart. He smiled at her as his hand caressed the silky smooth skin beneath his rough fingertips. Even a few weeks ago, Kat would have moved her leg away, reluctant to give him even that much control. Now, she might hesitate for an instant, but without a word of protest or even a question, she relaxed even further, happy to have him in control, freeing her from any decisions

His hand kept moving until it reached the moist heat between her legs. The silk fabric was already damp from her arousal. His fingers slid under her panties, playing with the wet curls. Her ragged indrawn breath was more evidence of her arousal, as were the hard nipples pressing against the soft cotton of her shirt.

"Unbutton your shirt, Kat. Let me see what sexy lingerie you're seducing me with tonight."

She did not hesitate. Placing her now empty glass next to his, she untied the shirttails knotted at her waist, and began unfastening buttons from bottom to top. His entire hand was inside her panties now, his fingertips pressing against her clit, moistening it with the honey flowing from her. The breeze lifted the shirt away from Kat's breasts, teasing the hard peaks of her nipples, straining against the pristine white cotton of her bra. Her back arched slightly.

"Very nice. Unhook the bra." She complied, her eyes never leaving his face. When he was like this, when he was telling her what to do during their intimate moments, Rick's voice dropped an octave, becoming a harsh erotic whisper. His face hardened, too; only his eyes showed any emotion. He looked like a warrior in the moonlight, watching her like a guard watches a captive, knowing the extent of his control but ever wary of his prisoner.

Kat's pale breasts spilled from the bra as she unclasped the front hook.

"Take them in your hands and pinch your nipples. Hard." His voice was dark magic to her ears.

Kat's hands cupped her breasts. The contrast of her blood-red nails against her soft white skin mirrored the differences between them. Rick's ruggedness, her polish. His war-worn hardness, her war-torn fragility. A soft moan escaped her lips as she squeezed her nipples into throbbing peaks. Rick's movement in the creaky chair drew her attention away from her breasts to the outline of his erection, pressing against his jeans, highlighted by the bright moonlight. Kat was panting from the caress of Rick's fingers on her clit and the pinch of her own fingers on her nipples. She knew not to move against his hand. She had finally learned the lesson of remaining still until he told her what her next move would be. The first few times she had challenged him, he had withdrawn his touch until she stilled her movements. The last time, just days earlier, she had wrapped her legs around him without being instructed to do so. He had walked out of her apartment, leaving her naked and unsatisfied on the sofa.

Rick nodded his approval at her compliance and then shoved three fingers into her dripping pussy. Kat bucked as the orgasm hit her, taking her silently over the edge, her inner muscles squeezing his fingers, her hands squeezing her throbbing breasts.

Before she had time to catch her breath, he was standing before her. Unbuttoning his jeans, he grasped his penis in one hand and her head in the other. She needed no more instruction than that. Kat's tongue sneaked out to lick the drops of cum from the glistening head of his cock.

Her hands snaked around to hold Rick's tight ass as he guided his cock into the welcome heat of her mouth. He held her head in place as he fucked her mouth, just three hard thrusts, until his explosion poured down her throat and dribbled onto her chin. Wiping Kat's face with the tails of his shirt before he cleaned himself, Rick grinned at her, despite her breach of the rules. She smiled up at him, flashing a cat-like smile of satisfaction, that she had gripped his luscious ass in the heat of passion, without retribution. Bending, he swept her up into his arms. Her laughter hung in the night air. In a few steps, he had crossed the walkway and was at the water's edge. Kat could feel the spray from the breaking waves on her bare feet and legs.

"What did I tell you about touching me?" His face was stern in the moonlight.

Confused, she stared at him, thinking he must be kidding. He was not. "I didn't touch you. I didn't...oh, you mean, when I held onto your ass?" He nodded curtly.

"I was afraid I'd fall out of the chair if I didn't hold on."

"Do you really think I would let you fall? Haven't I told you that I won't let anything happen to you as long as you do what I say? You have to listen to me, Kat, and do what I tell you to do."

Chastened, Kat slowly nodded. Except for the bruises on her wrists from their first encounter, he had never left a mark on her, never really hurt her. And the sex had been even better than with Sam.

"I'm sorry, it won't happen again." It was almost painful to say the submissive words to him.

"It's late and I'm tired, so you get a pass tonight, Kat. But there will be punishment for your transgression. You will just have to wait for it." He laughed. "Or I could just dump you in the Atlantic Ocean right now. Which would you prefer?"

The splashes that were soaking her feet were damn cold. Kat had no desire to take a late night swim in the ocean in October. "I'll wait," she whispered, still only half believing he would really do anything. *It's not like he's going to spank me or anything*, she thought, as he carried her back to the beach house.

Katarina awakened early to the sound of the sea gulls and the bright light shining through the window of the second-floor master suite. She lay quietly in the big bed, taking in her surroundings, feeling a bit disoriented. The French door opening onto the second floor deck was slightly ajar so cool ocean air circulated through the room, the tang of salt air wafting over her.

Here too, the décor was stark white, accented by marine colors: turquoise, teal and navy blue.

The bed was huge, firm. And occupied.

Kat had not slept with anyone else in ten years. *Over ten years*, she silently corrected herself, because Michael had already been in Iraq when he died. She stiffened as Rick rolled from his back onto his side. *What the hell am I doing in bed with another man?* Having sex was one thing, but the intimacy of sharing a bed through an entire night was feeling like the ultimate betrayal of her dead husband.

OUT OF CONTROL: KAT'S STORY

Swallowing a sob, squeezing her eyes so no tears escaped, Kat was buffeted by memories of quiet Sunday mornings, waking late, making love with Michael, sometimes staying in bed all day with bagels, the Sunday *Times* and lazy kisses. Their first nights together—when they would awaken two or three times to make mad, passionate love—causing them to oversleep and almost miss Criminal Law class. Cool, rainy evenings when they fell into bed, exhausted from a long day's work, too tired to do anything more than kiss goodnight, mumble "I love you" and curl up in each other's arms, falling asleep within moments.

"If you move any further away from me, Kat, your very fine ass is going to end up on the floor."

Kat rolled over to face him. She could see Rick was propped up on one arm, staring at her. Rubbing her eyes and feigning a yawn as if she were just waking up, she gave him the lie. "I was scootching over so I could get out of bed to pee without disturbing you."

"No, you were putting enough distance between us so that your dead husband could fit right in here, next to you," Rick gestured to the two feet between them, "and boot my ass out of bed."

At the mention of her husband, the tears Kat had been holding back ran down each side of her face, dripping into her ears, forcing her to wipe them away with annoyed sweeps of her hands. When Rick gently asked her if this was the first time she had awakened in another man's bed, all she could do was silently nod *yes*.

"Listen, Kat, I didn't lose my wife to death, but I lost Elizabeth because of war. It was a long time after she left before I could spend the night with a woman without feeling that I was betraying her all over again—first, by leaving her alone so I could go off and do battle and second, by not staying alone myself." He reached out to brush away one of her stray tears. "I didn't know your husband, but from what little you've told me, he would not want this war to take your life away, too. When Elizabeth remarried, it about killed me. But, I still loved her enough to want her to be happy. I expect your husband would feel the same way about you."

When fresh tears began to fall, Rick gathered Kat into his strong arms and just held her, until she feigned sleep. She felt Rick's body alternately tensing then relaxing, as if he were fighting a war with his own memories. Finally, he extricated himself and quietly climbed out of bed. Only then did Kat succumb to sleep.

Kat awoke a short time later to the smell of breakfast cooking. She wandered downstairs wearing Rick's cast-off shirt. He was in the kitchen making omelets. She came up behind him, carefully wrapped both arms around his waist and whispered, "Thanks."

Rick turned around and planted a chaste kiss on her forehead. "You are welcome. Now, go fix us something to drink, darlin', while I finish these eggs."

In his honor, Kat made Salty Dogs and set the table on the deck.

The weather was balmy for October at the shore. The sun was hot, and the Atlantic was not so cold that she couldn't get her feet and ankles wet. And she did. Both of them had dressed in jeans and sweatshirts over their swimsuits for their walk along the beach after breakfast. Kat's hands were full of shells and beach glass. Rick meandered beside her, matching his long strides to her shorter ones.

"You have some pretty cool shells in your place. I bet they didn't all come from here."

"A lot of the beach glass did, but you're right. The conch shells are from the Outer Banks. Most of the rest came from beaches in Indonesia and South Africa."

"Is there any place you haven't been?"

"Hmmm, let me think, the North Pole and Antarctica."

What am I doing with this man? Kat liked him way more than she had expected to. She had thought they would have a hot and heavy fling when she first agreed to go out with him.

But after he tied her hands, she wanted more of his domination. He was so comfortable in his skin, so even-tempered, so interesting, and sometimes so sweet. And so damn handsome, with the wind blowing his hair around his chiseled features, his eyes the same color as the autumn sky, squinting at the sun-dappled waves. And those clever hands tucked into his jeans pockets. He was the picture of the world-weary adventurer, contemplating his next voyage. For a moment, he looked so sad. Throwing caution to the wind, Kat wrapped her arms around him in a fierce hug.

Rick lost his balance for a moment, seemingly startled by her actions. His arms swept around Kat as he took a step then stumbled in the soft sand. Down they both went, Rick twisted to cushion her fall, and Kat landed on top of him. She pushed up, her hands on his shoulders, laughing down at him. He had a stunned, somewhat bemused look on his face.

"Time out, okay?" Kat asked, as she began lowering her mouth to his. "Time out from all the touching and controlling rules. Let me kiss you. Just once."

Before Rick could answer, her lips were on his, wet and warm. Kat caressed his mouth with the tip of her tongue until finally he swept his hands into her cascading curls and took her mouth with a crushing kiss that ended with him on top of her. He broke the kiss by rolling off her, stretching out beside her on the sand, a stunned look on his face.

Silently, he helped her to her feet. Walking back to the cottage, he kept her hand in his until they reached the deck. When she went inside, Rick walked around to the front of the cottage. Some strange noises came from the garage and in a few minutes, Kat heard him call to her. She found him sitting in an ancient navy blue MG convertible in the driveway. Squealing her delight with the classic car, she scurried down the stairs.

"Hop in, baby, let's take her for a spin." She didn't need to be asked twice.

"I love this car! Where did you get it?" She ran her hands over the pristine leather seats.

"Twenty years ago. I got it in Florida when I came back from South America. Drove it up the coast. Found this little cottage for sale on the Jersey shore. The rest is history." Rick reached over to squeeze her neck, pulling her to him for a quick, hard kiss.

They drove the short distance to the northern tip of the island—past houses still being rebuilt, and the last vestiges of Hurricane Sandy. Talking and holding hands, they spent the rest of the day strolling around Barnegat Lighthouse State Park. Tired and wind-burned on the ride back to Rick's house, Kat assured him that it had been one of her best days ever.

"Let's finish the day with dinner out. I know a nice place. Wear something sexy, will you, darlin'?"

Hours later, stuffed from a fabulous meal at Bisque Restaurant, Rick steadied Kat as she climbed the steps to the deck. One hand carrying the vanilla crème brûlée she just had to order but couldn't eat, his other hand wrapped around the slightly inebriated woman's waist, Rick was laughing. It had been a really good day, and it wasn't going to end. Yet.

Once inside, Kat dropped her bag on the nearest chair. She spun around, arms outspread, her colorful wrap draped over both arms, she imagined them flying out like butterfly wings, as she enjoyed her alcohol-induced lack of inhibition. She hummed some silly song off-key. She sensed Rick's burning gaze on her and she stopped spinning and stood, still, just watching him. The fire in his gaze ignited a burning desire deep within her. The wrap dropped from her arms but still she stood, swaying slightly, never taking her eyes from his face. The simple black dress she had worn for the evening wrapped her in nightshade, long sleeves, scoop neck, draping gracefully to her slender ankles. Desire, then confusion, then determination flashed across Rick's face.

"Take off your panties, Katarina. Now." He leaned back against the kitchen island. The rough command of his voice thrilled her.

She swallowed hard at the dark and deep sound of his words. She started pulling her long skirt up both legs, until she knew he could see the scrap of black silk at the apex of her thighs. Her fingers slid under the elastic on both her hips as she pushed the panties down, bending at her waist and letting the length of her dress fall back in place. She rose, stepping out of the tiny pile of black fabric.

"That was quite a nice show, darlin'." He gestured to her undergarment. "Pick them up. And turn around."

She did as he instructed, the panties dangling from one hand. She turned and faced the sofa, her other hand resting on the soft twill slipcover. Rick stepped up behind her. His hands slid down both arms and he pulled her hands behind her.

"I'll take these." He removed the panties from her grasp and, holding both wrists together, he bound her tight with the black silk and elastic.

Rick pulled Kat's shoulders back, her long French braid bisecting the black dress, ending just above her bound hands. He gave the braid a sharp tug and Kat let out a ragged breath, part pain and part anticipation.

"You didn't think I had forgotten about last night and what you have coming to you, did you?"

A shudder of fear and, to be honest, anticipation ran down her spine. Rick's hand was still grasping her hair, his other hand still holding her bound wrists. She could feel the hardness of his erection pressing against her ass. *What did he have in mind?*

"Ummm, no, but I hoped you had." She turned her head to shoot him a sideways, playfully pleading glance, a slight smile playing around her lips.

"Sorry to dash your hopes, but I warned you about the rules. It is time to 'pay the piper' as the saying goes." Rick's hands were moving up and down her torso, stroking her shoulders, breasts, and her hips. Kat could feel her nipples tightening as his hands swept over them lightly, caressing her. She sighed and pressed herself back against him. Before she could say anything, she was bent over the back of the sofa, Rick's knee nudging her legs apart.

"Oh, no, Katarina. You move when I tell you to move. Understand?" She nodded her head affirmatively. He was only going to fuck her from behind, not punishment at all as far as she was concerned. Rick was not like Sam, he varied their positions. Kat never knew how or where sex was going to happen between them, but it was always mind-blowing and almost always involved her being bound or placed in a position where she could not move. Giving that level of control to Rick had only smarted a bit in the beginning, and now she loved the freedom from decision-making her capitulation had afforded her. And the pain. He was right. It took her mind away from any experience she had shared with Michael. Pain freed her to feel the pleasure Rick gave to her. A small smile played around her lips.

He tugged sharply on her braid. The smile left her lips, replaced by a slight grimace and a groan. Her eyes met Rick's, emotions swirled in those cerulean depths. Kat wanted to answer the questions she saw there, pain, guilt, yearning, pleasure. She wanted to give him what he wanted, because he was giving her what she needed. But she didn't know what to do because, *damn*, he was taking away her ability to form a coherent thought.

His hands gripped her dress. He began sliding it up her long white legs, over the swell of her hips and her round ass. Her tush bared, he stepped back, leaving her momentarily bereft of his touch. Rick bent and ran his tongue along the cleft that separated her twin globes. She moaned. Her nostrils flared at the scent of her arousal, the sweet musk of the wetness that was already pooling. Rick bent and bit one cheek, just a nip, before he stroked a finger where his tongue had been, and lower. Through her thick folds. Kat moaned again, tilting her ass up so his touch went deeper.

The sound of the slap cracked through the silence like thunder. Kat jerked up in pain. And humiliation. Her father had spanked her on a few occasions when she was a rebellious young girl. She had hated it. She threw Rick a fulminating look that shot daggers. His hand was already stroking the red mark on her bottom.

"You still don't get it, do you? I told you to be still. But you can't control yourself. That first one was for moving just then. The rest will be for last night. And for you."

"For me? I hate being spanked." Kat could not imagine why he thought she would feel anything positive about being spanked.

"Were you spanked as a kid?"

"Yes, a few times. I hated the way it made me feel, embarrassed and humiliated. And it hurts."

"I know. But this will be different. Trust me. You need to learn who is in control. And you need to trust that I will make you come. Do you trust me?"

She nodded.

"Use your safe word if it gets to be too much. But, it won't. You and I need this." His voice dropped to a barely perceptible growl. "And you want it."

Rick pushed her down over the sofa back again, still rubbing the spot his hand had connected with on her ass. He pushed her legs even further apart and then stepped closer to her left side—she could feel his erection against her hip and he was so hard. Still rubbing her ass, he let his fingers drift down to her clit and away. His hand came down in a sharp slap. She yelped, and his fingers moved into her nether region while her butt was still stinging from the slap. Rick was rubbing over the smarting skin, taking away the hurt, spreading the warmth. Again, on the other cheek. The smack on her ass, the caress between her legs, the rubbing on her skin where the slap still smarted. Then again. And again.

Kat was moaning now. But not from the pain. Every slap caused a clenching in her pussy, a flood of wetness that dewed her inner thighs and tightened her nipples. Part of her brain was telling her: *Kick him. Turn around and stand up. Tell him to go fuck himself.* But her brain was also reacting to the pleasure pulsing through her, the tension caused by her position and her bound hands, whispering to her. *Stay. Surrender. Come.*

Rick smacked her bottom for the fifth time, harder than the last. But this time, he didn't caress or rub the aching skin. This time his fingers slid into her pussy, three fingers curling into her, pressing her most sensitive flesh. She could feel the orgasm starting, deep in her womb, rushing vibrating through her.

Then his hand slid out of her, just as the tremors had begun. She heard the slide of his zipper, the soft thud of his belt hitting the floor and then the tearing of the foil packet. She was already gasping when his cock rammed into her. Holding her hips immobile, he fucked her. Hard and deep. His balls were slamming into her, hitting her pleasure point, pushing her to her limits.

He stopped again. Just short of her coming. She could hear him sucking in deep breaths like a stallion approaching the finish line, the sound as harsh as the breakers on the beach just outside the window.

He lifted her, turning her in his arms. His mouth crashed down on hers, his tongue invading her mouth with the same deep strokes as his cock had invaded her pussy. It didn't seem as if he could get enough of her. Rick's big hands gripped her ass, sitting her on the edge of the sofa back.

"Wrap your legs around me. And hold on." One hand held her head, his mouth still on hers. One hand gripped her ass. His cock was wet and hard between her legs as he pushed himself inside her. Kat had to encircle his hips with her legs, to hold her balance and to take him deeper. She had never been fucked like Rick fucked her that night. It was as if the ocean had broken over the dune and was crashing around her, into her. Wave after wave of pleasure swept over her, as he pounded into her like the Atlantic pounding against the shore. She screamed his name as his mouth left hers. Then she went limp in his arms.

Still cradled against his chest, but now unbound, the sound of Rick's whispers were the first thing Kat heard when she came back to herself.

"It's okay, you're okay. Baby, you're okay." He was rocking her.

Kat giggled weakly at the unlikely circumstances: battle-scarred ex-Marine babying tough litigator. They were not two people to whom comfort came easily.

"So, you've come back to life?" Rick looked down at her with a wry smile playing around his lips, but concern deepened the blue of his eyes to midnight.

"What was that? I don't think I've ever passed out from sex. Or do you think it was all the alcohol?"

"Probably both. Haven't you ever heard of *la petite mort*? It's what the French call the 'little death' meaning an orgasm so forceful that a woman can lose consciousness for a few moments."

"Well, damn, that was pretty amazing, Marine." Kat grinned at him as he pushed the tendrils of hair from her sweaty face. "I don't think I would want that to happen every time I came; I would never accomplish anything else at all." They both broke into laughter, at ease with each other, totally satisfied sexually and still a little intoxicated.

"Can you stand? 'Cause I think I'm done here." Rick eased himself out of and away from her. She looked down at the mess her dress had become, bunched around her waist, her bra and panties on the sofa, and sighed.

"I'm not sure, so catch me if I fall." Kat's smile was tentative. She slid off the sofa and wrapped her arms around his neck to steady herself. It was then she noticed the storm clouds gathering in his eyes.

"Hey, are you okay? Damn, was I not supposed to touch you just now? I thought that was only during sex. Some of your rules are more complicated than the Court of Appeals' rules."

"I'm fine. You're fine. I was just thinking that you have a warrior's heart, even though you carry no scars. Well, none that are visible anyway."

"You have plenty for both of us." Kat slowly traced the small scar above his left eyebrow, the raised welt of scar tissue that ran down his side, angling toward his naval. She knew there were three circular scars on his back, near his right shoulder, that could be bullet holes or burns. And those were only the scars she could see.

"I should give you a medal for your courage and daring." He threw her a mock salute in the midst of buttoning his shirt. Kat stilled as she pulled the front of her dress up to cover her breasts, at least. "I have medals," she said in a small, emotionless voice. "At least, I mean, I have Michael's medals. You get a Purple Heart for being killed in action. I guess they consider being blown to pieces by an IED being killed in action. There are some other ones, too." She sighed and then raised her head to look around. "Where are your medals? Are they in Cambridge or do you not have them on display anywhere? I have Michael's in a drawer in his dresser."

"They don't give medals for the kinds of battles I fought in, sweetheart. They just send you off for some R &R before you get shipped off to the next shit storm." Rick held out his hand to her. "Let's go to bed. We should both sleep good tonight."

Rick was right. They slept late into Sunday morning. After a leisurely breakfast and a long walk on the beach, they packed and cleaned up the cottage, working comfortably together.

Kat was relaxed and humming off-key. She sensed Rick's eyes on her every so often and she could have sworn he was engraving her image on his mind.

OUT OF CONTROL: KAT'S STORY

After tossing the garbage bags in a battered aluminum trash can at the side of the garage, Kat was surprised to see Rick slip the key to the front door under a loose brick at the base of the stairs to the deck. At the sight of her quizzically arched eyebrow, he shrugged his shoulders as they walked to the Jeep.

"I have another set in Cambridge. But in the past there were times when I was coming here from someplace else, someplace where I was not carrying keys. I want to always be able to get inside easily. Don't tell, okay?" He winked at her as he put the Jeep in gear and slowly pulled away from the cottage.

Before fastening her seatbelt, Kat made an *X* over heart. She would keep his secret and any others he might share. And she found herself hoping he would share more of his past with her, even as she fretted about the complications of a future with Rick. She needn't have worried.

CHAPTER NINE

As suddenly as it had begun—and with as little warning—it was over. It was early November, and Kat would still find herself staring into space, wondering what had happened and why she had not seen it coming.

Their drive home on Sunday afternoon had been pleasant. She had napped a bit, but mostly they chatted about New Jersey and New York, the things they liked and the things they loved about each state: seashores and mountains, Manhattan and Atlantic City, Springsteen and Billy Joel. They parted at Kat's apartment in the early evening with promises to see each other the following weekend, probably using Rick's Cambridge apartment as a stepping off point for a drive and possible overnight in the Adirondacks. They spoke on Tuesday night and all was well.

So Kat was completely taken aback when he called Wednesday evening and asked if she were busy.

"No, I just got in. It was a late day at the office. I'm just heating up some soup before I crash in front of the television."

"Well, I was in the area and I thought I might stop by." His voice sounded a bit strained. Kat looked down at her ratty sweatshirt and black leggings. Her make-up was off and her hair was already in its nighttime braid. Not her most attractive look. But he had seen her first thing in the morning, in bright sunlight, so what the hell.

"Sure, come on over."

When he buzzed her just a moment later, her worrying began. She was standing in the open doorway when he got off the elevator. "What's wrong?" was out of her mouth before he had even walked into her apartment.

"Hello to you, too." He bent to kiss her quickly as he entered. He had something behind his back and when she turned to him after shutting the door, she found herself staring at a huge pot of garnet mums. "I thought these would look nice on your kitchen counter, they match your red coffee mugs. I saw them when I stopped by the Farmer's Market on my way down to Troy."

"Thank you. They are perfect. But what brought you to Troy this afternoon? I thought you were writing today."

"I did. I mean, I was writing this morning. Then I had to come to Troy."

Kat remained motionless by the door, the feeling of dread beginning to coil in her gut. She did not let her feelings show on her face, schooling it into the emotionless mask she wore in court. But, she was aware of Rick's pained expression, the slump in his shoulders and the ring he was twisting and twisting on his finger. Whatever he had come to tell her—something so important it had to be said in person—was obviously so distasteful that calm, cool, in-control Rick was fidgeting. That realization softened her expression as she resigned herself to hear what was surely going to be bad news.

"Come, sit down. Do you want some soup? Some wine?" Kat headed for the kitchen, wanting something to do with her hands.

"Wine would be great, whatever you've got."

She poured him a glass of red and then resumed her seat on the sofa. Instead of sitting next to her, Rick sat in the leather chair that was adjacent to the sofa. *Zack's chair* was the thought that popped into her mind. She shook her head as if to dislodge the thought. This was not going to be good. Kat took a long sip of her wine. Rick did the same.

"I got a call this morning from the Coast. From LA."

"From your son?"

"No, from the guys I was working with in Toronto. They need me to come out to do some more work on that project, and they have something in the works that they need me to consult with them about." Rick did not look happy about the news.

"That's good, that's interesting." *Why is he so nervous?* It was just work.

"Yeah, it is. I like working with them. It sounds like a good project. So, I called my son and told him I would be in LA. He invited me to stay at their place. Ricardo got on the phone and started jabbering about something to me. I couldn't figure it out because he mixes his Spanish and his English with his baby talk." Rick smiled for the first time since he had entered the apartment.

"Wonderful. You must be so pleased you'll get to spend some time with them. How long will you be gone?" The smile immediately faded from Rick's face. He took another sip of wine before he looked at her.

It's over. It was written on his face as clearly as if the words were tattooed on his forehead.

"Well, Kat, I don't know. I may be gone for some time, for several months or even longer. I might even head out to Southeast Asia when I'm finished to look up some old colleagues. So, I wanted to come to see you so I could...." He looked away.

Well, that stings. She had thought there was something between them, something more than the sex. But, even so, she knew in her heart that she was not in love with him. She might have fallen in love with him, given the chance, but she was not there yet. Kat smiled, a bittersweet smile, and tried to ease his obvious discomfort.

"So you could say goodbye. That's really nice of you, Rick. I appreciate the flowers and everything. I hope you have a wonderful time with your family. I would say that I'll see you when you come back, but we both know that I'm not going to see you again, am I?" Looking somewhat relieved and very resolute, Rick took Kat's hands in his.

"No, you're not. You could have a life with someone, Kat, you're almost ready to love someone again. But, I'm not. I never will be. I'll be honest. I am beginning to care about you way more than I thought I could, but it will only go so far and then I will fuck it up. That's what I do, and I am not going to do that to you. So, I'm going to go to LA and do some work. I'll hang with my son and his family. And I am going to try to forget you. And I will forget you, or enough so that I can move on. That's what you need to do, too. Forget me." With that, he rose, pulling her to her feet. After a fierce hug, he was gone.

There was a card attached to the flowers he had brought. *Use the cottage on the shore as much as you want this winter and next spring, I probably won't be back until July Fourth. The cottage has always helped me heal. Rick*

Kat missed the next two days of work. She felt blue and alone. She admitted to herself she had liked Rick. A lot. Could she have loved him? *Maybe.* She didn't think so. She still didn't think she would ever really love a man again. But, hugging herself alone in her big bed at night, she had longed for him.

Shaking herself out of her reverie, she looked around his cottage. She had hopped in her Volvo and headed down to the shore on Saturday morning, the first weekend of November. The keys were where Rick had left them. The cottage was empty of any trace they had been lovers there for an entire weekend less than a month before. She took a long walk on the deserted beach, bundled in a jacket, hat, scarf and gloves against the angry wind and spray coming off the Atlantic. The ocean looked to be in as much turmoil as she had been since Rick left. Staring at the glowering sky, the spray mixing with the tears on her cheeks, Kat let herself mourn what would never be, what could never have been, with Rick. And then, she let her feelings for him go. She would be grateful for what they had shared, but she would survive. She had survived the abyss that Michael's death had made of her heart, so she could survive anything. Feeling as though a weight was lifted from her, she climbed the stairs from the beach and went back inside.

The main purpose of her visit to the cottage rested on the sofa where she had left it. A small mahogany box, velvet lined, held Michael's Purple Heart medal. For injuries or death sustained in war. Tucked under the box was a sheet of folded stationery. On the heavy gray paper, she had written, *To Rick. For gallant service above and beyond the call of duty, in honor of all your scars—seen and unseen—this medal is yours. You are an officer and a gentleman— and I will never forget you. Kat*

She turned off the lights and locked the door. One last long look at the beach and ocean and she was gone.

CHAPTER TEN

"What are you going to do now?" Mia demanded. They were at Jack's Restaurant for lunch a few days after Kat's trip to the shore.

"What do you mean?" Kat wasn't eating her butternut squash soup so much as she was aimlessly stirring it around the bowl.

"Don't be such a lawyer! I understand from what you've told me that Rick is in the wind, and there is no chance that anything further is going to happen with him. You crossed Sam and his very interesting, though certainly unattractive marry-me-and-we-will-climb-to-the-Court-of-Appeals-together offer off the list. Are you going to bury your head in the sand again or are you going to move on?"

Mia had held Kat's hand through the early days after Michael's death and then had nudged her back into the land of the living. It had also been Mia who had picked Kat up at her office the Monday after Kat had walked out on Sam and taken her to Garcia's for frozen margaritas while Mia ranted and raved over what she described as Sam's bizarre marriage proposal. Armed with her famous spaghetti sauce and all that went with it, including a huge bottle of Bardolino, Mia had been at Kat's apartment the day after Rick left. She knew when her friend needed cuddling and when she needed a boot in the ass.

"I don't know what I am going to do." Kat glared defiantly at Mia. Mia was undeterred; she circled her hand at Kat, as if to say *Continue, what's next?*

"All right, Mia. I do know this. I am not going back to my celibate lifestyle. How about that?" Kat folded her arms over her chest and glared at her friend.

"Bravo! Are you going to ride the trains some more? Maybe to New York? Or are you going to go online?"

"Very funny, though I do have an argument in the First Department next week so I'll be on Amtrak to the City." Both women laughed. "No, seriously, I don't think I want to go online. What if I hook up with someone we do business with, or someone we went to law school with? Yuck."

"Jeez, you might run into *Zack*."

"Seriously? Zack is still online?" Kat knew Zack had been into Internet dating years before, but thought he had stopped using online dating sites over the past few years. But, she realized, she really didn't know where Zack was meeting his "lady friends" as he described them to her. Come to think of it, Kat didn't really know very much about the details of Zack's love life.

"Zack is all over, honey. He's a player, in the nicest sense of the word." Mia laughed and continued, "I mean, you know Zack. He is definitely a 'love them and leave them' type of guy, but he does it with a great amount of panache, so they don't even shed a tear. And, of course, he does give them all marvelous parting gifts." She bit into her sandwich and simply raised an eyebrow at Kat's bewildered look.

"Zack buys them off, is that what you're saying? I don't believe it." Seeing Mia's knowing smirk, Kat fumed, "How come I don't know this shit?"

"Did you ever ask him? No, you don't ask Zack much of anything, except who the Yankees are going to pick up in the off-season, whether this lawyer is moving to that law firm or if he wants to go to a movie."

"I ask him about his love life." Well, Katarina had. And he told her about this nurse or that librarian. But he never gave her names or many details. And every time she had asked, it had been a different woman.

OUT OF CONTROL: KAT'S STORY

"Yeah, recently you have, but for years, he's just been your old friend Zack. To me, he has been a source of many titillating tales of dating adventures and misadventures.'"

"Well, who is he seeing now? The last he told me was that he was going to try dating a psychologist." Mia almost choked on her water at that announcement. Kat had to giggle at her friend's reaction. Then they were both off in gales of laughter at the notion of Zack dating anyone who had the training to see past his polished surface.

"Zack would no more date a psychologist than he would date a lawyer. Way too easy to let down your guard with another lawyer, way too easy for a shrink to analyze our beloved but very commitment-phobic friend." Mia found her voice first.

"What are you grinning about, Mia? You know something. You look like the cat who swallowed the canary." Kat hated to be left out of a secret.

"Well, I swallowed something this morning, but it wasn't a canary." Mia licked her lips.

"Oh my God, spare me your smug references to married morning sex." But Kat was smiling at her dear friend. Mia always made her laugh, was always a font of gossip and good advice, and had been there for her through every crisis of the last 13 years. She was as good a friend as any woman could ever want.

"Mia, I just feel like I want more. I want more sex." Her voice dropped to a conspiratorial whisper as Jack's became more crowded. "But, you know, not just another lover. He will have to be a man who could do what Sam and Rick did...and maybe a little more."

"Katarina, my love, I think you are going to have to look online for that. But be goddamned careful. There are a lot of sickos online. Hell, there are a lot of sickos walking around Albany. And our classmates have defended most of them."

They laughed in unison again and signaled for the check.

"I just don't know how you are going to find a man with the particular...skills...you are looking for. It's not like you could walk up to that guy over there, for example," Mia waved a finger toward the rather handsome man in a suit sitting at the bar, "and ask him if he is into whips and chains."

And the two women were off into snorts and giggles again.

Their discussion kept repeating itself over and over in Kat's brain for the next few days, until she was having dreams about a masked man with whips and chains, and when she pulled his mask off, it was Zack.

Early Sunday morning found her at the gym, working into a sweaty mess on every available piece of equipment. After a quick shower and a change of clothes in the ladies' locker room, she walked out into the hall. Fishing for her keys, she was not looking where she was going and bumped into a solid and sweaty male.

"Ooops, sorry." Kat looked up. "Zack! What are you doing here?" She blushed as the whips and chains immediately popped into her head. And, of course, it didn't help that Zack looked all male and athletic in his sweaty gray T-shirt and black shorts.

"Jeez, Kat, you almost knocked me over." Zack shrewdly examined Kat's face, as though looking for some hint as to why she was so preoccupied that she had run into him. Kat chastised herself. It wasn't like her not to pay attention.

"You know, it was *my* gym before it was yours. I came over to work out like I do every Sunday." He poked her in the shoulder—which hurt like a bitch—and said, "You would know that if you showed up here with any regularity." He waved at a tall, equally sweaty man who brushed by them "There was a basketball game starting so I decided to shoot some hoop with the guys instead."

She was giving him an exasperated look.

"What's up?"

OUT OF CONTROL: KAT'S STORY

Kat stuck her tongue out at him, as she usually did when he was annoying her. But this time, Kat caught Zack's intense focus on her mouth, and the slight change in his breathing.

"I was working out and I am here regularly. Just not religiously, like you. You're such a jock." Kat straightened her bag on her shoulder and continued. "Anyway, I was going to get some bagels. Do you want me to bring some over to your place? It's on my way. I'll even get you coffee."

She had not been to Zack's place in some time, what with work and family. And dating.

After her conversation with Mia, she decided it was time for her to catch-up with her old friend.

"No need to bring coffee, I can make it, and your tea, at my place."

"Okay, I'll be there in like 30 minutes. So hurry up. And take a shower."

Zack lived in a condo on the second floor of a beautifully restored brownstone not five minutes from Kat's apartment. Arms full of bagels and cream cheese, she rang the bell by the front door, 35 minutes later—parking in Troy seemed impossible even on a Sunday morning. His voice drifted over the intercom. "Come on up, the apartment door is unlocked."

"I need to work out more," Kat mumbled breathlessly to herself as she trudged up the long flight of stairs to the second floor. But the climb was worth it. Even the foyer and staircase in Zack's building were gorgeous with old wood and brass sconces, including a chandelier illuminating the entire entryway. Kat's tastes were more modern and a bit eclectic but she could appreciate the beauty of the period pieces that Zack adored. She just wasn't crazy about all the damn stairs.

Kat let herself in and wandered down the hall to the kitchen. Dumping the bags on the counter, she could smell the coffee that was brewing. Zack loved old antiques, except in his kitchen. There he had every modern food preparation tool available. Dark-brewed coffee was dripping from a fancy coffee maker into its carafe. A high-tech one-cup brewer was sitting on the granite counter, a box of individual tea flavors open next to it. *No way am I touching that. Why can't he just boil water like the rest of us? And where the hell is he?*

She stepped into the dining room and then moved to the living room. Zack was nowhere to be seen. Kat circled back to the hallway and called, "Zack! I'm here. What the fuck are you doing?"

The door to his bedroom at the end of the hall swung open and there was Zack, clad only in a huge white towel, covering him, waist to ankles, but leaving his chest bare. *Damn.*

"I had to straighten up a bit first so I just got out of the shower. I'll be dressed in a minute." The door closed.

"Well, don't bother on my account." She was muttering to herself again. The man had her muttering all the time, it seemed. And since when did the sight of Zack's bare chest affect her? *I've been swimming with him in the pool at the gym and in the pond at the farm. I've seen his chest before. His very broad, well-muscled, slightly hairy chest, with that little line of slightly darker hair running down the middle all the way to...* She shook her head as if to clear it and busied herself in Zack's kitchen, slicing bagels and setting the small café table by the window that looked out into the private courtyard the three condos in the brownstone shared. The trees were bare and the brick pavers were swept clean of leaves. Stark and cold, waiting for winter. A chill swept over her.

"Hey, what are you looking at?" Zack's voice made her turn from the window. The man lived in gray. Gray sweatshirt with faded garnet letters spelling out *Union* across his chest worn over faded blue jeans, frayed to almost gray at the knees. Heavy gray socks on his feet. The same socks Michael had worn on cold weather weekends. A small, sad smile tugged at her lips. She always felt closer to Michael when Zack was around.

"Are those new socks or are you still wearing the ones you and Michael bought in bulk when Cramer's Armory went out of business?"

"Still wearing them. You can't kill these socks, you know that. I think I still have a few pairs that I haven't even worn yet, they're still in the package, in the back of a drawer somewhere." Fixing her cup of tea, he paused. "Is that why you were looking so sad when I walked in? Thinking of Michael?"

"Yes and no. Winter coming on always makes me sad. I don't mind the snow or even the cold so much as I mind the lack of color. Everything looks dead."

"Well, that's because it is, dopey. Or at least it's dormant. But, think how much you love spring. It's your favorite season. All your favorite colors come in spring." He pointed at her outfit.

Zack knew her so well. Kat looked down at her black leggings, topped by an amethyst tunic over a red turtleneck— her striped socks picking up all those colors and more. Even her running shoes, left by the door, were red, purple, lime green and black. Her good spirits restored, she sat down and began smearing her sesame seed bagel with cream cheese.

"So, why did you have to straighten up? Didn't your cleaning lady come on Friday?" She eyed him suspiciously over her bagel. "Or did you have someone here last night? One of your lady friends?"

"Yes, Missy came on Friday to clean, and she said you've not been home a lot lately because there was nothing much to clean up at your place." They shared the same cleaning lady, the same dry cleaner, the same gym, and the same synagogue. The same past. "I had the poker game here last night, Miss Nosey Pants. I needed to take out the pizza boxes and beer cans."

"Did you win? You know the wives get pissed when you beat Dick, Joe and Donnie. You have to let them win sometimes." Michael had been the only one of their law school classmates who made up the poker group who could beat Zack with any regularity.

"I did okay, but Donnie did better. Damn inscrutable Chinese face of his. It's like trying to figure out what a statue of Buddha is thinking." They laughed together. Their friends from law school had not changed over the years. Still a tightknit group of funny, smart, tough, goodhearted men, all of whom had become successful attorneys, though Donnie was probably the most successful due to the major real estate deals he had brokered over the last ten years. Joe was a Town Judge in a small Rensselaer County town and Dick was a partner at a large Albany firm specializing in labor law. Zack, with the skills he had honed in the District Attorney's Office, had become the area's premier criminal defense attorney.

"It's a sad state of affairs when you are playing poker with a bunch of married men on a Saturday night instead of going on a hot date with one of your nurses or flight attendants." Kat smirked at him. Mia was so off base. Zack was not gallivanting around with all these hot babes as she had implied to Kat.

Nonplussed, Zack drawled, "I was out with an opera singer on Friday night. She had a performance last night." Kat almost spit out her tea. Zack just grinned and reached for more cream cheese. "She was in town for *Madame Butterfly* at Proctor's Theatre. I know her from summers at Lake George. She's buxom and blond and sings like an angel."

"Mia was right, then, you are a player." *Why does it sound like an accusation?* "I mean, I know you date a lot, but Mia said you are a ladies man who loves them and leaves them."

"Well, I certainly make love to them. Or, at least, many of them. And we part company, as you well know, because none of them are living here. I'd like to think it is by mutual agreement and no one's feelings are hurt in the process."

Kat just sat and stared at him, speechless. Why was she so relieved to hear there was not and had not been anyone special enough to tie Zack down? And why was she so pissed at the notion of several, many, maybe legions of women, traipsing through Zack's life, sharing his bed?

OUT OF CONTROL: KAT'S STORY

Zack, too, was silent. Kat's eyes latched onto his, and the battle of wills began to see who would look away first. It was Kat. Her ire had cooled, but she was irritated by the number of woman Zack had likely been with. And even more pissed by the darts of jealously that she was experiencing.

"Of course, it really isn't my business." Kat replied stiffly. "I just thought you would settle down someday. I mean, all of your friends are married."

"You're not." Kat softened a bit at that. She had been happily married, and she really did want that for Zack.

"Yes, but I was. And you should have children so there is someone to carry on your name."

"So should you." Zack had frequently voiced the opinion that Michael and Kat would produce the most beautiful children. Remembering his oft-repeated remarks, Kat felt a momentary tug at her heart for Michael's children she would never have.

"I have nieces and nephews who will carry on the Galchinsky and Kaufman names, so the pressure is off me. You're it for your family."

"I adopted a duck at a rescue farm in California. His name is Diego Reichman. So I do have a namesake." As always, he made her laugh.

"Okay, I give up. You're such an asshole." She kicked him in the shin, her good temper returned.

"Yes, but you love me." Zack flashed his shit-eating grin.

"I do, damned if I know why."

"Because I love you, even if you are a pain in the ass."

Their relationship seemingly restored to its normal balance, Kat and Zack lingered over the bagels for most of the morning. But, Kat could not seem to shake the feeling that something had changed between them.

Over the next couple of weeks, they were thrown together again and again. They celebrated Hanukkah with Kat's family on both the first and last nights. Bubbe had admonished them both about the weight they had lost, scolding them about their busy lives that left them no time to eat. She piled their plates with extra potato latkes and dollops of sour cream and applesauce, and sent both home with containers of mushroom barley soup and rugelach.

There had been an awkward moment when Bubbe had seated them next to each other. With all the family at the table, Kat and Zack were wedged so closely together, Kat could feel his leg pressed against hers, knee to thigh. Every time he moved, she felt an odd flutter in her belly. Trying to ignore the feelings fighting in her, Kat had inadvertently taken too large a bite of a sour-cream-laden latke. Before she could use her napkin, or even lick the excess sour cream from the corners of her lips, Zack's finger had snaked out to sweep the creamy white stuff away. Gasping from the unexpected intimacy of his touch, Kat started to turn away so he would not see the flush she felt creeping up her cheeks. But, not before she saw him suck the sour cream off his finger. Her nipples had hardened at the sight of his tongue, causing her to blush even more furiously. For the rest of the evening and the entirety of Hanukkah, she kept thinking about Zack's mouth and how his tongue might feel on her lips.

Zack and Kat were together again at the annual alumni Union-RPI hockey game, with a group of classmates, cheering on their alma mater as the Dutchmen beat the Engineers. That reminded Kat of the early years of their friendship, after being with family and classmates, all of whom loved Zack. Sitting with everyone in Zack's living room after the game, sharing stories of their victories and defeats in Moot Court and the early years of their careers, brought Kat back to freshman year.

She had suddenly remembered the Freshman Keg Party in the Courtyard of the law school. She was sitting on one of the picnic tables. Michael had gone to get her another beer and Zack was sitting next to her. She was singing a drinking song from college, totally off-key as usual, making Zack and the others gathered around burst into uproarious laughter. She laughed so hard that, in her inebriated state, she started to fall backward. Zack's arm had caught her.

"Easy now, Kat. I've got you."

His face was so close to hers and his eyes had looked so beautiful, she had swayed slightly toward him and whispered, "Yeah, but what are you going to do with me, now that you've got me?"

Zack had grinned so sexy and superior and leaned in to kiss her—she was sure he was going to kiss her—when Michael had arrived with their drinks. Zack and Kat had pulled apart and Kat now remembered feeling oddly put out with Michael for interrupting the intimate moment. *How had I forgotten that?* It made her once again wonder about kissing Zack.

She had resolved to put aside her conflicting, troubling thoughts about Zack and just enjoy their time together. It certainly was not as though anything was ever going to come of all those crazy, erotic thoughts.

CHAPTER ELEVEN

"Ceci, I'm leaving now. I have to get over to the VA Hospital for that board meeting at five," Kat called though the door of her office as she was pulling on her coat. It was mid-December and the temperatures were dropping. Snow coming in for the holidays.

Ceci looked up when Kat stopped by her desk. Bundled up in a black wool coat, black boots, gloves, Kat's red hair and red scarf were all that saved her from looking like she was dressed for Halloween.

"I know. I have it down here in your book. And don't forget that you have a dentist's appointment at eight tomorrow morning. I guess I'll see you around ten?"

"More like nine-thirty; it's only a cleaning. As long as it doesn't snow, I should be here by then. Otherwise, who knows?" Kat stopped to look out the window at the lights from the cars on State Street. "Drive carefully. It's so dark out already. God, I hate driving in the dark." Her arms full with briefcase and purse, Kat breezed out of the office and into the elevator.

At five minutes before five o'clock, Kat was walking through the front doors of the Albany Stratton VA Medical Center. Before she could juggle her black briefcase to grab the door, a long arm, swathed in camel hair, reached out and pulled the door open.

"After you," came a deep voice from behind her. Kat stepped into the lobby and turned to thank her benefactor.

"Thank you," came out of her lips more like a sigh than an expression of polite gratitude. *Tall, dark and handsome* looked down at her from at least six feet tall. Kinky curly dark brown hair, chocolate eyes, full lips and an aquiline nose, with café au lait skin, were her first impression. Second, he was a big guy, not husky, but big-boned, broad shoulders and large hands. He was delicious.

"You are welcome. Those doors weigh a ton and that wind sure doesn't help." His voice had just a bit of Southern molasses, low, slow and rich. Strike three and she was out, definitely feeling the hots for *tall, dark, handsome with a sultry accent.*

"They aren't easy even in good weather, so thank you." She had regained her composure. "Have a nice evening," Kat said as she turned toward the bank of elevators.

"You, too." The stranger responded as he followed her to the elevators. They both got on the same elevator and reached for the third floor button. Their brief ride was in silence. Kat turned right to go to the ladies room and *tall, dark and handsome* went through the doors to the left.

When she entered the conference room a few minutes later, Kat was more than a little surprised to find him sitting at the long table. He was wearing a thin black turtleneck under a black blazer, with gray flannel trousers. His long legs were crossed at the ankle and, damn it, he was wearing grey argyle socks with his black wingtip loafers. *Why do argyle socks always give me butterflies in my belly?*

He glanced up and smiled when she entered but continued chatting with the two other Board members sitting across from him. Kat left her coat and scarf on an empty chair and sat at the end of the table where she could spread out the papers that were necessary for the meeting. As *pro bono* legal counsel to the organization servicing local homeless veterans, she always had the most documents when they met. *Tall, dark and handsome* had not taken his eyes off her. They were dressed practically the same; that morning Kat had donned a similar black cashmere turtleneck to wear under a plain gray wool jumper that just skimmed the tops of her tall black leather boots. Her mass of hair was pulled back by a black leather headband.

The chairman of the organization, Dr. Charles Randall, greeted her.

"Katarina, I'd like you to meet our new member, Bradley Robillard. He's the representative from Calvary Church on State Street. Brad, this is Katarina Galchinsky, our counsel and a long-time Board member."

"Pleased to meet you, Ms. Galchinksy." Bradley rose and extended his hand in greeting. Her hand was lost in his large warm one. And she felt that telltale tingle as he squeezed her hand once before letting it go.

The other two Board members had arrived and the meeting began. Bradley was the new deacon and alderman at Calvary Church, having recently relocated from Baltimore. But he was a hometown boy, Albany born and bred. From what Kat could ascertain from the conversations going on around her, he had graduated from Albany High School and joined the Army. After four years, he had left the service and attended college on the GI Bill. He was a bit of an entrepreneur in the technology field, earning an MBA from Yale and quite a lot of money along the way. But, abruptly, it seemed, in the past year, he had sold his company and returned to the Capital District, where he became affiliated with Calvary Church.

Soon, Kat was packing up her papers, duly approved by the Board and signed by the Chair. A new soup kitchen was in the works at Calvary and additional beds were arranged for the shelters in Troy and Schenectady, to prepare for the increased numbers of homeless veterans forced off the streets by the onset of winter in the Northeast. Saddened by the numbers of men and women who had served their country but now had no home, Kat was silent as she reached for her coat. Once again, that long camel hair-clad arm reached around her.

"Let me help you." His voice was like a song from the South, zydeco and magnolias rolled into one.

"I'm fine, really."

"My grandmama would skin me alive if I did not offer to help a lady on with her wrap. Her ghost will haunt me tonight if you don't let me do what she taught me. Please don't let her disrupt my dreams." He held her coat up so she could easily slip into it.

"Well, I know about grandmothers and their rules, so thank you again, Mr. Robillard." Many times Bubbe had popped up in her head, scolding her with her arthritic finger about some transgression or omission.

"Call me Brad, please, Ms. Galchinsky."

"It's Katarina, or Kat, if you prefer."

"I've always had a fondness for cats, so Kat, it is."

They walked out into the cold starry night together. He continued with her to her car. She turned to say good-bye, but he spoke first.

"Kat, I hope you don't mind me being a bit forward, but do you have any plans for dinner tonight?" Kat tossed her briefcase into the backseat while she considered his question. It had been two months since Rick had left for the West Coast. There had been no contact between them. Despite Mia's suggestion she look for prospective dates online, Kat had not done so. She had spent the time thinking about Rick, thinking about herself and thinking about Zack. No answers had come to her, except she was becoming very much in need of some rough-and-tumble sex.

"No, I don't mind and no, I don't have any plans. Do you like pizza?"

Within fifteen minutes, they were walking into the back door of The Fountain, a law school hangout that still made the best pizza in Albany. Once again the gentleman, Brad helped her off with her coat. She did not think she imagined the way his long fingers grazed her neck as he eased her coat off her shoulders. Squeezed into a booth, his long legs kept bumping into hers under the table. By the time their pizza arrived, Kat was feeling edgy and needy from the constant contact.

Brad told her he had been married and was now divorced, with one daughter, who was attending college in Baltimore. He admitted it was his work that had driven his wife and him apart. She had resorted to a series of affairs to fill the loneliness of the days and weeks he had been away on business.

"She threw that in my face when she asked for a divorce. I had no idea. I was that absent from my marriage. I gave her what she asked for and it was plenty. Fortunately, I had received a great offer for my business. I sold it and split the profits with her. She and my daughter will always be comfortable."

"Is that why you left Baltimore?"

"Partly. And my mother was ill here in Albany, so it seemed as if that was a sign for me to move back home. She is doing better now, but it was touch and go for a while. I was spending a lot of time in church, praying for her, praying for direction. I got to know Reverend Gardner at Calvary Church. When he mentioned that they needed a deacon and an alderman, someone handy and someone who knew business, I knew that was my answer, at least for now. It doesn't pay much, which is not an issue for me, but I do get a pretty amazing apartment in the church."

"Seriously? You live in the church? Isn't that a little strange?" Kat could not visualize such an arrangement.

"It was at first, but my apartment is on the second floor, near the offices and classrooms. And, I have a spectacular stained glass window in my bedroom." Brad reached out to take Kat's hand, his finger stroking down the palm. "Would you like to see it?" The man was smooth, and direct, she would give him points for both.

"Tonight? I don't think so, not tonight. But maybe some other time." Kat was definitely interested, after the quiver of desire shot through her when he stroked her palm, but she was not quite ready to traipse around a Methodist church with *tall, dark and handsome* in the middle of the night.

Brad just smiled and kept stroking her palm as their conversation moved on to other topics.

It was freezing when they left the restaurant to walk to their cars. Kat unlocked the door to the Volvo and once again, turned to say goodnight. Brad smiled that knowing smile of his and bent to kiss her. He held her face in his big hands and gently brushed his lips over hers. Kat sighed at the sweetness of the kiss. It was all the encouragement that Brad seemed to need. She had been shivering from the cold but as his arms encircled her and he deepened the kiss, the heat of his embrace almost scorched her. He held her arms to her sides by his hug and she was helpless in his hold. The kiss seemed to last forever. They broke apart only when they heard voices coming from other patrons exiting the restaurant.

"I'll call you in an hour." Brad said as he helped her into her car. "I have your number from the meeting. Drive carefully, Kat."

Her ride home did nothing to calm her nerves and her needs. Was it possible that Brad was the next one? The one she had been wanting since Rick's abrupt departure, the one that would keep the troubling dreams about Zack at bay?

"Katarina, are you all tucked in?" Brad's deep voice inquired exactly sixty minutes later.

"Yes, I'm in my jammies, under the comforter. All alone in my big bed."

"Is that what you prefer, being all alone in your bed?"

"Not all the time, not anymore."

"I see. Well, I don't think a beautiful, sensuous woman like you should be alone ever."

"What are you proposing, Deacon Robillard?"

"I would like us to share more than our mutual concern for homeless veterans, more than just conversation and a kiss, although I can still feel that kiss, counselor."

"I would have to agree."

"Good, but I have terms." *He had terms? What the hell was this, a merger negotiation?*

Brad continued, with his deep sexy voice caressing her ear. "It would not be fair to you if I didn't explain that I have special…needs…when it comes to intimacy. Obviously, safe sex comes first, I am sure you would agree. And exclusivity. But more than that, I have a need to…control…our intimacies. Do you understand what I am saying?"

"Yes, you want to use condoms and we don't sleep around; I agree with that. And as for the other, does it involve whips and chains?" She meant that last as a smart-ass remark, but his indrawn breath and whispered words in French made her worry she had perhaps shocked him.

There was a long moment of silence, and Kat wondered if she had gone too far.

"Do you like whips and chains, Katarina?" His voice was dark with desire.

"I don't know. I don't think so."

He murmured as if disappointed with her answer and then said, "Well, I don't usually resort to whips and chains on a first date, but I have been known to use restraints. And clamps." Kat sucked in her breath, *yes!*

"And I require a certain degree of…submission, Katarina. Do you think you can do that?"

"Yes, I do. I need to cede power in the bedroom. I want to do that."

"And shall I spank you if you disobey me?"

Now, it was her turn to pause, to consider. She had rather enjoyed Rick's spanking lesson. The pain from the slap and the resulting heat emanating across her bottom had been mightily arousing.

"If you must," Kat whispered.

"Well, then we have a good beginning. I'll speak to you tomorrow night. Sweet dreams, Kat." And then he was gone.

In the dark of her room, in the comfort of her bed, Kat pondered the direction her life had taken. She had been alone for so long, lost in sorrow, then ensnared in her belief that to honor Michael she must not love again. And she had not loved anyone since Michael. Giving herself up, to the power of her lovers, had taken the decision-making out of her hands and had allowed her the freedom to have sex again. The physical pleasure Sam gave her was so different from what she had experienced with Michael that sex with Sam had never felt like a betrayal. Rick had tugged at her heartstrings more than a little. Kat thought perhaps that it was because he had served in Iraq, like Michael. Rick, too, had suffered losses, like Kat. *And, he was right, pain as part of the sex was a counterpoint to the pleasure I still feel a little guilty about craving.*

Whips and chains and silk scarves wrapped around her wrists filled her dreams that night. Restless and unrested, Kat woke in the early morning darkness, wondering, as she had when she fell asleep, *what did he mean about clamps?*

CHAPTER TWELVE

It didn't take long to discover what Bradley wanted from her. Kat agreed to a Saturday night date after two more evenings of telephone conversations ranging from the ongoing violence in the Middle East to the chances of the Baltimore Orioles to capture the pennant in the next season to the extent of Kat's experience with BDSM. Bradley managed to cajole her into describing what she liked and didn't like from her encounters with Sam and Rick.

"My dear Kat, it seems there is still a good deal for you to experience and learn in this area. I would be delighted to teach you. And I believe that you will be a very good student."

"I had straight As in college and was on *Law Review* at law school. I am an overachiever. And a quick study."

"Then we'll have a delicious dinner on Saturday and a delightful time after, getting to know each other." She could get drunk on the whiskey timbre of his voice.

"Is that 'know' in the Biblical sense, Deacon?" They both laughed at that. They had laughed quite a bit since their nighttime conversations had begun. Brad was interesting and funny. But, his voice could slip into dark and dangerous without warning. Kat would feel herself get wet, when he caressed her desires with his words. She couldn't help but wonder what the real thing would be like, both wanting and dreading the experience at the same time.

Brad arrived at her door promptly at seven o'clock Saturday night, looking even more gorgeous than she remembered, in black jeans topped by a black sweater over a white dress shirt. His black leather jacket was open, but he wore a beautiful black and brown scarf draped around his neck. In his hands was one long-stemmed red rose.

She took the rose from him after planting a soft kiss on his cheek. He just smiled at her. As she walked toward the kitchen area, Brad let out a long low whistle. Kat knew then that she had chosen her outfit for the evening correctly. Her black leggings tucked neatly into tall black suede boots. What appeared to be a simple cowl neck tunic of copper and black in fact, dipped low in the back, revealing creamy white skin. She had gathered her hair in a messy topknot, tendrils curling on her neck and falling around her face. For adornment, she wore only large copper hoop earrings and several bangle bracelets.

"Sugar, you don't disappoint. I will give you that." Brad's voice vibrated with desire.

"So you say. So you say." Kat smiled and handed him her black suede parka. They decided to walk to Daisy Bakers even though December's chill was on the night; with no wind, the walk was pleasant. Especially with her hand tucked into the crook of his arm.

Brad loved the old townhouse feel of the restaurant and the pork belly on the menu, although he couldn't tempt Kat to try it. They enjoyed bourbon with their appetizers, the warmth of the alcohol bringing an even deeper flush to Kat's cheeks. Brad's eyes were full of dark promises. In a secluded corner, they touched surreptitiously, knees and feet, fingers entwining then breaking apart. By the time Brad called for the check, Kat was a vibrating mass of need.

They walked home quickly under the sky dotted with stars, the moon hung low over the river. Nervous, Kat could find nothing to say in the elevator. Brad just watched her with sexy speculation in his eyes.

"Can I make you a cup of coffee?" She asked after she hung their coats on the hooks in the entryway. A glance at the hooks had her remembering Rick. She swallowed hard. *What could Brad possibly have in mind?*

"No, but thank you. Katarina, come here."

She hesitated.

"I'm not going to bite."

"Oh, damn, I was hoping you would." Kat smiled, hoping her smart reply would ease the tension she felt. *No such luck.*

"Kat. Come here." Brad waited by the windows.

She approached him slowly.

"What do you think is going to happen here?"

"I'm not sure. I don't see any whips and chains." She looked around.

Brad pulled her into his arms and laughed. "Nothing is going to happen that you don't want. But if you can trust me, much will happen that I think you need. And I need too. You just give me your safe word and we will stop. What word do you want to use?"

"Safety," she whispered

Brad laughed again, then tipped her face up to his and kissed her.

Kat once more felt overpowered by his strength and his passion. Swept away on a crest of passion, she reached up and looped her arms around his neck.

He broke the embrace. "First lesson, Kat. When we go through the doors to your bedroom, or when we are in mine, you don't make any moves I don't give you permission to do. And you are silent unless I give you permission to speak. Except for your safe word. Understand?"

Kat nodded silently. She knew her eyes had widened at his words but she hoped the trepidation she felt was not evident in her gaze.

"Good girl. Now go into the bedroom and wait for me."

She stood quietly by her bed. A calm had come over her as she walked through the door, as if the control she had ceded to Brad had also taken the weight of responsibility off her shoulders. Brad was there in minutes, a small satin bag in his hands.

"No whips and chains, Kat, but a few accessories you will like. Now, let's get you out of those clothes." He relaxed in the chair by the window.

"Boots first. Then leggings, then sweater." He watched intently as she disrobed, dropping her clothes in a heap on the floor.

She stood facing him clad only in cream lingerie, festooned with black satin bows. Her chest was heaving with her growing excitement, and her nipples were hard against the silk of her bra.

Brad rose and walked to her. His long fingers traced the edges of her bra before they slipped beneath the silk to pinch her nipples.

She gasped when he flicked open the front clasp. Cool air hardened her nipples even more. She looked up at him. Brad's eyes were watching her reaction carefully.

He reached into the bag he had left on the edge of the bed. Two silver, beaded clamps were in his hands. "Take your bra off." It fell to the floor.

"Lift your breasts in your hands."

She flushed slightly at the command but complied without hesitation. He fastened first one clamp and then the other to her swollen, erect nipples. The pinch hurt for an instant, but the pull of the weights sent a sensual message to her pussy. Kat could feel the answering swell in her nether lips, the slow drip of her mounting passion. Brad bent and gave her a quick kiss on each peak.

"Now the panties. Pretty as they are, we don't need them anymore." The silk bikinis joined the growing pile of discarded clothing on the floor.

Brad motioned for her to lie down on her bed. While she did, he swept the pillows to the floor, except for one, which he placed under her ass. Surprisingly, Kat felt no embarrassment to be naked and open before this man. He was supremely self-confident and in control. And his eyes showed just how pleased he was with her easy compliance. And the bulge in his jeans showed Kat just how much he wanted her.

His long fingers reached out to sweep along her cleft, dipping into the honey between her legs. He smiled and licked his finger. Once more, he reached into the bag. Long silken strands wrapped around his fingers. Watching her intently for a negative reaction, he wrapped one around her left wrist, knotting it snugly and bending to wrap it around the leg of her bed. He did the same with her other wrist. Smiling at her raised arms and splayed legs, Brad removed his sweater and tossed it on the chair. Then he wrapped and secured her ankles to the legs of the bed.

She lay spread-eagled before him. "Are the bonds too tight?"

She hesitated.

"You can answer me."

"No, they're fine."

"No, they're fine, *Sir*."

"They are fine, *Sir*."

"Very good." Brad kicked off his boots and socks. With his eyes locked on Kat's, he unbuckled his belt, unzipped his jeans and let them drop. His legs were long and well muscled, tan and smooth. He unbuttoned his shirt and tossed it on the chair. His chest was broad and also smooth. His erection was huge within his black silk boxers.

Kat smiled and licked her lips, like a cat about to enjoy a bowl of cream.

"Why are you smiling?"

"I like boxer shorts on men, *Sir*."

Shaking his head at her impertinence, he ran his hands up her legs till his thumbs met at the junction of her legs. The smile left her lips on a deep sigh.

"I don't much care for hair here, Kat. But we will make do tonight. After this, I expect you to be clean-shaven." When her eyebrows flew up questioningly, Brad answered, "Don't worry, I will take care of it. No one is touching this sweet pussy but me." He bent and placed a hot kiss on her mound, as his fingers spread her even more. Kneeling at the foot of her bed, he smiled at her one more time and then his dark head was between her legs.

His mouth was like fire on her clit. His tongue licked her as if he was the cat and she were the bowl of cream. Then his teeth nipped her clit. The spark of pain was enough that her ass came off the bed. But not far enough, tied down as she was. He stopped and gazed at her, his lips slick with her passion. Watching her, he slipped one long finger inside her vagina, then another. Twisting them to find her pleasure point, Brad bent once again to his task. The sensations licked along her nerve endings. She moaned while he ate her, and he was moaning, too—the delicious vibrations adding another layer of pleasure. When he pushed a third finger into her, his mouth never leaving her clit, the orgasm crashed into her. Kat felt as if she were imploding, her hips bucking and writhing, her bound wrists and ankles holding her down. She wanted to be loose, to grab his hair, to climb on top of him, but not as much—she realized through the aftershocks—as she wanted to lie on her bed and let this powerful man take her.

Before she could catch her breath, Brad was shoving another pillow under her butt. Her back was arched, her pelvis tilted up. Taking all the time in the world, Brad removed his boxers. *Oh. My. God.* He had the biggest cock she had ever seen, long and thick and completely without hair. There was a drop of cum on its tip. Brad sauntered over to the side of the bed. He pulled her head toward him and rubbed his cum on her parched lips. When she stretched her neck to be able to take him into her mouth, he jerked her head back by the hair.

"Not unless I give it to you, Kat. And as much as I would love to watch you suck my cock, and you will, tonight I just want to fuck you. You can scream if you want." His thumb traced her lips before he moved away.

After sheathing his enormous erection in a condom, Brad gave the nipple clamps a tug. An answering throb spiraled up from her soaking wet pussy. Climbing between her legs, he ran the head of his cock around her clit, before he positioned it at the entrance to her aching vagina.

Slowly, slowly he slid into her, stretching her. Kat's breath was coming in short pants as Brad filled her. She was sure she could not take all of him, but he kept pushing into her. Braced on his arms, touching her only where their bodies joined, he loomed above her.

Brad lowered his head to kiss her, his tongue invading her mouth; Kat could taste the salt and sweet of her pleasure on his lips. His tongue moved in and out of her mouth, fucking it with the same rhythm that his cock was fucking her pussy.

She moaned.

Abruptly, he rose up onto his knees. Brad pulled her hips onto his thighs, never stopping his thrusts. The new angle drove him deeper into her, and she could feel another orgasm beginning, curling up from her womb, causing her legs to vibrate with the explosion that was to come. He was tensing too. She could feel the muscles in his thighs tighten, saw his eyelids begin to droop as his climax approached. Almost there, Kat's body was arching, her eyes were closing, her breaths were coming fast, when he pulled the clamps from her nipples. Pain shot through her, combining with the exquisite agony of her orgasm, till she was screaming his name.

Coming back to herself, drifting in the post-coital afterglow, Kat was dimly aware that Brad was freeing her wrists and ankles from their restraints. As much as she wanted to stretch her limbs then curl onto her side, Kat lay still. Not sure of the protocol in this new relationship, she was uncertain whether any movement on her part would earn her a reprimand. She didn't have to ask. Brad pulled her head to his chest, wrapping an arm around her, smoothing strands of hair from her sweaty brow.

"Are you all right, Kat?"

"Yes... *Sir.*"

"Very good, Katarina. You were magnificent. I knew you would be." Brad planted a kiss on her tousled hair. "I wanted you from the first time I saw you, striding across the parking lot, looking determined, but also a little lost. I watched you all through the meeting and sensed you might make a proper submissive, with some training. And the training can be so rewarding, so pleasurable. You've passed your first tests with high marks, counselor."

"Thank you, *Sir.*" Truthfully, Kat was getting a bit annoyed with the use of the word "sir." But, as she lay in his arms, relishing the feeling of having her brains fucked out, she considered that, for now, it was well worth it. *But would it be enough?*

CHAPTER THIRTEEN

Brad's bed floated in the middle of the large, nearly empty, room. Fat white pillows like pale cherubs clustered at one end, the fluffy white comforter made it look like a cumulus cloud. The scene of the seduction was set. Colors spilled through the rose-shaped, stained-glass window, dappling the floor with amber and azure, carnelian and crimson, indigo and violet. He had prepared the stage, every detail seen to and embellished. Not just a cold beer, but Corona with lime, not just snacks but the crisp radishes and smooth Gouda cheese Kat preferred. On the good china, with linen napkins.

Music wafted from the bedroom, a mix of Country, Zydeco and Puccini, designed to relax and arouse her. The lights were dimmed to set the stage for the next level of seduction. Of submission.

On one of the console tables next to the bed, there was a steaming bowl of water balanced on a pile of towels, shining stainless steel razor and soap sitting next to it. All this was as it should be, as it had been since the first time over three weeks ago when Kat first climbed the broad marble steps past the gargoyles and church bulletins, to the Deacon's apartment. Above the choir loft and the sanctuary below. A bizarre location for a lover's tryst. But part of the affair's appeal to her.

Kat found Brad to be a man of God, one of the fallen angels, like Lucifer. He spoke of his love for the church. He professed his desire for Kat. Kat thought she was a constant temptation to his devotion, to his avowed commitment to make himself a better man. Kat did not love him, but she had encouraged his desire because right now she needed him more than he needed God. In her lonely life, she had controlled everything for years. She had been learning to lose control, no, to give up control, first with Sam, then Rick and now with Brad. He was the most demanding. Kat smiled to herself. *Admit it, Katarina, he is the most domineering.* With him, she had not just given up control in the bedroom; she had submitted to him. In his bedroom, Bradley bid and she obeyed.

Kat had arrived as instructed at Calvary Church precisely at six o'clock. There were no meetings, no choir rehearsal on Thursday nights. It was icy and cold outside. Albany was in the grips of late January's frigid temperatures and heavy snows. But that day had been sunny and almost mild. Snow had melted from the streets and sidewalks, her path into the church was clear. But, she wore her black mink coat, her hands still encased in leather gloves when she knocked on Bradley's door.

It wasn't long before he removed her coat, and placed her gloves and scarf neatly folded next to her purse. She had taken a chance and left her boots in the car, hoping he would appreciate the new dark blue spike heels she had balanced precariously on as she picked her way across the church parking lot.

"I've been waiting for you all day, sugar. It seemed like forever to get through all the paperwork I had today. I couldn't focus, I kept thinking about what I had planned for you tonight."

Kat's stomach gave a little flop. Up till now, she had been excited and aroused by Brad's increasing demands and introduction of new rules, restraints and implements. But each time they were together, she felt as if a little more of her identity was slipping away. His demands were reaching beyond the bedroom and insinuating themselves into other areas of her life. They were meeting three times a week: Monday, Thursday and Saturday evenings. Always at his apartment. He called her at eleven each night, on the landline at her apartment, so he could ensure she was home. In bed. Alone. At first it had seemed like a harmless adventure. Now, she was beginning to chafe. Not enough to leave, just enough to make her edgy, just enough to make her want to disobey.

She smiled at him as she reached for the beer and for Brad. Here, still beyond the boundaries of the bedroom, she could reach for him; she could pull him close, and whisper all manner of naughtiness in his ear. "I've been thinking of you, too. That's why I bought these shoes. I thought you would like them. And what goes with them." She nipped on his ear.

Brad lifted his head and seemed to stare straight into her soul. His smile was amused.

Amused and a little annoyed.

"I got you something, too. A new toy for our collection."

She turned back to the bedroom. There was something new pillowed on the downy white.

Something small, something pink.

Kat turned back to him with a raised eyebrow and a question in her eyes. He smiled and nodded, gesturing her toward the bedroom.

Permission granted, she entered the inner sanctum. Stopped. After one last pull, she put the beer on the other table by the bed and then started her transformation by taking off the dark blue suit jacket, draping it on the small chair adjacent to the dresser. He watched silently from the door. Brad always watched without comment, at least since the first time when he had instructed her in his ways. Next came the slim skirt, neatly folded upon the chair. The pale blouse slipped from her arms, a whisper of blue silk, placed on top of the skirt.

Clad in only snippets of lace and nylon and high blue heels, she turned to him, waiting.

He nodded. Sometimes he wanted her in those scraps of lingerie. And the fuck-me heels.

Sometimes, naked for his pleasure.

"Leave on the nylons and the shoes, sugar. I do love those high heels."

Kat reached up to unclasp the bra with shaking fingers. Her last moments of any control slipping rapidly away from her, as she slid the panties down those pale legs he sometimes loved to wrap around his shoulders as he ate at her delicate flesh.

Not yet. She turned and stood quietly, back to him. Ripples of anticipation running through her. Then he was behind her, pressed against her momentarily, his cock already so hard she felt him throbbing through his pants. Feeling him, she reached up to sweep her long auburn hair away from her neck. Waiting.

Soft, smooth leather. Black leather. Small silver rivets placed evenly round the collar. From the buckle dangled a silver heart. Engraved. *Lawyer bitch*. Its weight settled coolly on the base of her neck. One of her first gifts from Brad. He had laughed with some amusement at a story she had related to him in the first days of their relationship about a car salesman who had become frustrated with her negotiation skills when she bought her Volvo. Instructed by his manager to make the deal she wanted, he had walked her through the delivery of the car. Only to slam the door and call her "lawyer bitch" as she drove away. "No one else had ever called me that, at least not to my face. I couldn't stop laughing. I kind-of liked it, it was a like my super hero name: Lawyer Bitch, Defender of the Defenseless. I almost had a T-shirt made to wear at the gym." The next time she met him, he had presented her with the collar. Now, she wore it every time she was in his bedroom.

Brad motioned her to the bed. She sank gracefully onto the fluffy white, sweeping her arms out and away from her body, posed as if to be crucified on that bed.

He grasped her ankles and spread them wide, wider still; she flinched at the pull of muscle high up in her inner thigh. He smoothed his hands up those quivering legs, ankle to pussy. Stopping just short of her pleasure, pressing his thumbs in where the flesh quivered.

Soothing and inflaming her. She moaned; he smiled.

Lifting her hips, she waited. He pulled a towel from under the steaming bowl, sliding the thick terrycloth under her ass. Kat sank back into the nubby softness, reaching for one more sip of beer, while he looped the restraints at each corner of the bed around her ankles. Pulling them tight, he left her, spread-eagled across the comforter.

At the head of the bed, he reached under the coverlet for the silken restraints that would hold her wrists. He looped one over her left wrist and pulled it tight, securing her. Stepping around the bed, he did the same to her right wrist. The music continued echoing from the living room. At times, Brad would sing some of the words, while he made sure Kat was secure.

"Are you warm enough, Kat? It's a bitter night out."

"Yes, I'm fine. Thank you for asking, Sir." Brad smiled and stroked her hair, pleased with her respectful response. She rotated her head into his palm, like a kitten seeking her master's hand. But, he smacked lightly on her cheek, the reprimand clear. No nuzzling unless he gave permission. Besides, there was still work for them to do.

That first time they had sex, he had remarked on the auburn curls covering her pussy, attesting to the fact that she was a true red head. He wanted unimpeded access to her sweet nether lips and her clit. As much as he loved fucking her, he told her after, he loved eating her more. Kat had promised to make an appointment to get a complete wax of her pubic hair, but Bradley insisted on shaving her himself. On her first visit to his apartment, he had done just that. Shaving her pussy was his special gift to her, his special mark on her. It was like nothing she had ever experienced before.

Hot water, creamy soap, the cold steel against her overheated, swollen flesh. She ached for this each week. The surrender, the risk, the sheer eroticism of spreading herself for him, the clean feel of her pussy when he was done, the lotion he smoothed on her, musk rising in heated waves from her body. The sweet chaste kiss he planted on her mound when he was finished. Kat gave herself up to the sensations, to the pleasure of her bonds. Of being readied for him, knowing what was to come.

Wait. *Wait.* No words, no sound could escape her lips. The waiting was the hardest.

Then she heard a sound. Not from her, not from him. It was a soft purring sound. Mechanical. She lifted her head to see him smiling up at her from between her legs. He clasped something small and pink in his hand. The item that had been on the bed before. She laughed, then immediately bit her lip. Brad smiled at her. "That is okay, Katarina. I know you are surprised by this, but remember, I told you that the Japanese made vibrators in the shape of cartoon characters, even Disney characters. You didn't believe me. Well, here she is." He held the toy up for her inspection. *There was Hello Kitty*, smiling at her, clutching her teddy bear, perched upon a pink column of desire. Vibrating.

"Hello, Kitty. H-e-r-r-r-o-o-o kitty!" he said.

Pink and pretty. Small, disappearing into his large hand, but she could hear the whirr of the vibrator. Palming her pussy, he pressed the toy against her, its indentations fitting her in an uneasy but arousing fashion. She could feel his fingers, she could feel the hard surfaces, she could feel the vibrations touching her.

He bent to her pussy, touched her clit gently with his tongue, licked from top to bottom.

Where was Kitty?

Kitty was sliding into her pussy, head first, ears scraping her slick passage. *God.*

Sprawled across the bed, legs spread wide for him, she was still. The vibrations from Kitty were reverberating through her pussy. Pleasure spreading through her nerve endings, into every part of her body. She wanted to coil in upon the pleasure, but she couldn't move, unless bidden by him.

How could such a small toy pulse with such incredible power?

Brad watched her, the heat creeping up her belly and across her breasts. The fingers of her restrained hands were flexing. Her head tilted back a bit, exposing her long throat. Kat could feel his smoldering eyes on her, watching, assessing her level of arousal. She let her tongue snake out to lick her lower lip. She was barely able to contain the pleasure from Kitty that flowed through her vagina to arouse her whole body.

Brad reached down and gave the small bit of Kitty still protruding from her cunt a quick twist.

Jesus! It was a prayer and a plea, exploding from her lips. Her eyes, which had been drooping closed at the lovely sensations, flew open and locked on his. He laughed. "You like your little pussy toy?"

She murmured her assent.

"Can you purr like Kitty?"

"Yes. Sir." She whispered.

"Purr for me, darlin' and I'll make you come."

She sighed and a low sound escaped from her throat, a purring sound, a moan, a wish.

Please.

She was dripping wet. She always got so wet when he shaved her, the pleasure and the anticipation arousing her to new heights each week. She knew Brad could see the silky cream slick on her bare pussy lips. She wished she could see her dark pink nether lips, accented by the light pink plastic tail clasped tightly between.

Brad bent and took a deep breath. "I love your scent, sugar, that unique mix of soap and sex, wet and woman."

Her hips were starting to move, a slight flexing, a soft thrust. Long legs pulled against the restraints. He laid a hand on her belly to still her.

"Please, *Sir*." He raised an eyebrow at her breach of bedroom etiquette. She would have to pay for that.

"What do you need?" Brad's voice was a low growl.

"You. *Sir*." She was gasping.

"What do you want?"

"Your tongue. *Sir!*" *God, why did he play this game?* She was writhing with need.

"Where?" Brad's question was soft, almost casual.

"My clit. God, please lick my clit. Please. *Sir!*" Kat was almost sobbing as the vibrations from Kitty pulsed through her.

Bending, Brad grasped her thighs almost roughly and pulled. Pulled her legs even further apart. Open to him, offered for his pleasure. And for hers.

His hands pushed at her inner thighs, even as his fingers spread her pussy wide. Throbbing, the glistening center of her sex protruded. She loved him to lick her clit, slick and hot, loved him to suck it into his mouth, making her sob her pleasure. And when he held her clit gently between his teeth and flicked it with his tongue, she dissolved into a puddle of need.

All this he did to her. All this while Kitty purred inside her, held in place by his thumb.

Kat was melting. Her pussy. Not the hard plastic pussy vibrating inside her, its irregular edges poking into her soft tissue, tantalizing her. Her pussy was flowing with cream. She imagined in her fevered mind that Kitty was lapping up that cream, much as Brad was lapping up the juices that were running out of her and onto his greedy tongue.

The tremors began, softly, gently, from the touch of his tongue on her clit, and then spread through her, up her abdomen and down her legs. *God, God*!

Thrusting against his mouth, her movements hampered by the restraints around her ankles, she started to come. His hands held her tight against his mouth, held Kitty tight inside her, while he sucked her clit. Moans were rising in her throat, sliding out of her mouth, louder, louder, until she screamed in release just as he thrust a finger inside her. His long finger stroked her pussy and Hello Kitty, from the inside out, pushing against her silken, molten walls, pushing her up and over again, and again.

She was rocking, her whole body convulsing as she continued to come. He laughed his approval of her release, even as he removed his hands from her thighs and his mouth from her clit. Only Kitty remained. Inside her. Purring and vibrating for her pleasure. He slid up her body until his clever mouth found her nipple. He sucked. She bucked beneath him. He squeezed her other nipple, shaping it into a proud peak.

Her breath was heaving out of her in raw gasps.

His hand left her breast; his mouth did not.

He continued to lick her nipples, first one then the other, as his free hand brushed lazy circles on her belly. Lower and lower. When it slipped between her legs, he pressed up and against Kitty's protruding tip. And bit down on her nipple.

She arched up and into him, her breast thrusting into his mouth, her undulating hips rising into his hand, her cunt grinding against him.

Gasping, crying, screaming, she came again. A long, deep orgasm that rocked her back onto the softness of the bed, limp and wet.

One, two, three moments passed. He pulled Kitty out of her swollen cocoon, stopped the vibrations and dropped the toy on the towels next to the bed. The ankle restraints were next, but her legs remained splayed open. Her pussy lips felt slick with her cream and her sweat.

Breasts heaving as she dragged cleansing breath into her lungs, she opened her eyes.

He smiled and released her wrists from their bonds. She swiveled her head, making half circles on the pillow, easing the stiffness. Climbing up beside her on the bed, he reached for her.

She turned into his arms, laying her head on his chest as he stroked her back.

"There, my baby. There, my good girl."

It was only then that he held her, in surrender and in repose, as if his whole world rested in his arms as the rainbow of lights spilling across the room and their bed faded away in the onset of night. Kat came to him for the release only he could provide. She knew it aroused him to the point of insanity that she was his slave, if even for just two or three hours on their three evenings each week. Lying in his arms, Kat knew Brad wanted more and tonight he'd taken her further than ever before.

She could feel his hardness pressed into her belly.

"You can suck my cock now, sugar."

Kat reached out to undo his belt, unzip his jeans. He was naked inside the denim, and his penis pushed its way up and out as soon as she had the zipper pulled all the way down. There was already a drop of cum on the swollen head of his cock.

She licked her lips, moistening them, wetting them for his climax.

His hard, throbbing cock, rested against her throat as she playfully licked his belly.

Lower, lower still. The smooth tip of his pulsing rod was at her lips, her tongue licking up the first drops of his arousal.

Now she made him moan. He thrust against her mouth as she licked, circled the crown with her tongue, a small smile playing around the corners of her mouth. Her wet swollen lips surrounded the head of his cock, sucking him in centimeter by centimeter.

She took him down her throat, all the way in, until he was embedded in the warm wonder of her mouth. Her tongue swirling around his cock as she sucked. And sucked.

She felt him pressed against the back of her throat. Sucked again, continued sucking as she slid her mouth up his cock, from base to tip. Caught the tip in her teeth and swirled around the head again, more drops fell on her lips. He was swelling, growing in her mouth, heavier, thicker.

Oh, he's going to come. He was going to come so hard in her mouth, the creamy liquid would spill out and dribble down her chin, falling in steamy tears on her breasts.

But, not yet, not so soon. She loved to suck him, loved his taste, loved the surrender implicit in her act, But she loved more his submission in this instant, his trust in her, his reliance on her to bring him to completion with just her mouth. She reached out.

Hello Kitty. Kat's hand closed around the sticky plastic wand, still wet from her pussy.

Still sucking on him, licking him, she twisted Kitty and welcomed the purr she heard.

She looked up at him when he lifted his head, trying to keep the mischievous look out of her eyes. He raised an eyebrow. She smiled, innocent and pleading. He nodded.

Kitty purred in her hand. She pressed the clever toy behind his balls, already tightening. In that space between passion and oblivion. Were the vibrations flowing from Kitty to his ass and to his cock? He was gasping. A double delight.

And she continued to suck him, sliding up and down his cock, swirling her tongue around his stiff penis. Brad's hand found her hair, twining it through his fingers, tugging her head down on his cock.

Now. Yeah, now. Kat thought. Brad wanted her to finish him now. He always chose the time of his coming. Sometimes her mouth was barely on him when he erupted into her and onto her. There were nights when her jaw ached from sucking him before he would allow his release.

But when his hands found her hair and pulled, she knew he was ready.

She pressed Kitty higher, a bit higher, against the base of his cock. He jerked, involuntarily, and then swelled for the last time. His hand held her in place as he thrust into her, as he fucked her mouth, as he gave himself to her, and as she took him, deep, deeper, all the way to the base of his cock, Kitty vibrating against her lips.

Hot. So hot and so much of him spurted into her mouth. She swallowed once, the salty thickness sliding down her throat so she would taste him for hours afterward. Then again, more cum, too much, too much for her to manage, gushing out of her mouth, in twin streams, splashing on her neck and his belly.

Spent, Bradley fell back. Kat rested her face on his thigh. Her lips felt swollen, and she reached up to smear his essence around her mouth and chin. Her skin glistened from her exertion on his behalf. He stroked the damp auburn hair now, softly, brushing the mass from her face and neck. From the collar.

They lay together for several moments, the music wafting around them, Puccini playing now. Colored light from the stained glass window dappled Kat's supine body with rich color, as though buried in a pile of freshly fallen autumn leaves. At times like these, she felt supremely satisfied. Then Brad's long fingers tugged on her collar.

"Kat, get up."

She rose stiffly from the bed and stood quietly next to him. Brad reached out for one of the cloths and, wetting it in the still warm water, cleaned his semi-erect cock. He dropped the cloth on the pile of towels and reached for another. Motioning her to him, Kat bent so he could wipe the traces of his explosion from her face, neck and breasts. And he washed between her legs, lingering just long enough to tease her clit. Need vibrated through her.

"You can undress me now."

She quickly unbuttoned his shirt, removed it and his jeans from his smooth, powerful body. He had instructed her on her first visit to fold the clothes and place them in the basket by the door to the bathroom. Kat turned and started back toward the bed. His cock was swelling to almost full size. The man had a marvelous ability to recharge, and she was anticipating a good fucking at his hands. Maybe with the clamps this time.

Brad sat at the end of the bed. Kat stood before him. Moisture was gathering between her legs and her nipples were so hard they hurt. *Maybe the nipple clamps would not be a good idea.*

"You have made some mistakes tonight, Kat. You know you will have to be punished." *Oh, shit, what had I done? Rubbed my cheek against his hand? Had I forgotten to say "Sir" when I came?* Try as she might to remain passive, Kat could feel an annoyed flush creep across her cheeks, and her nostrils flared. Brad noticed her infinitesimal signs of defiance. He pulled her down across his lap and administered three quick slaps on her bottom. She jerked at each one. These were not like the smacks administered by Rick, sharp caresses that stung yet aroused. This was a "you've been a bad girl and I am boss" spanking. Tears sprang from her eyes, and she was about to speak, when Brad abruptly stood her backup.

"You need to go stand by the doorway now, Kat. Right now." He sounded really angry. Schooling her face into the picture of compliance, Kat was seething inside. Something of her anger translated into her walk turning it more into a stomp. At the door to the living room, she turned to face Brad. Displeasure played across his features, but arousal was evident in his erect and swollen cock.

"Kneel down." When Kat just stared at him, Brad repeated the command. She knelt awkwardly in her high heels and nylons still held in place by lacy garters encircling her thighs.

Her hands, resting on her those bits of elastic and lace, clenched into fists.

"Fold your hands on your lap, Katarina." She looked away, not wanting him to see the displeasure in *her* eyes. "Look at me when I am speaking to you," Brad barked. She did as she was told, silently fuming.

"I had wanted to introduce you to the next level of our relationship tonight as a way of heightening our pleasure and deepening our bond. But, now I see I must do it to show you who is in control here. Earlier, you did not wait for permission to touch me and you did not address me properly. You know there are consequences when you disobey the rules. You need to apologize. Now."

Kat considered telling him to go to hell but she wanted to just get through this, She did not want to have an argument about her limits while she was almost naked, stinking of sex, in his bedroom. Better to conduct that conversation during their nightly phone call or at least, once she was dressed and in his living room. "I apologize. *Sir*."

"Good girl. Now, you've been punished and you have apologized properly. We can move on to more pleasant activities." He had hardened noticeably when she said she was sorry. Brad reached down and began stroking his cock. It was huge in his hand. His thumb spread around the few drops of cum that glistened on its swollen head. She couldn't take her eyes off it.

"I want to fuck you, Katarina. I want you to come here and sit on my lap, wrap those long legs around me and take every inch of this cock into your hot, dripping cunt. Do you want that?"

Well, hell, yes. I want to be fucked by him. She was almost panting she wanted it so much. Her lawyer's brain rationalized that as long as she was there and wet and he was there and hard, it would be a shame to waste that beautiful erection. "Yes, *Sir*," she whispered.

"Then you will have to ask properly. You need to say 'Master, how may I please and serve you today?'"

Stunned, Kat simply stared at Bradley.

"Say it and you can have this cock inside you, fucking you until you scream."

Kat whispered one word: *Safety*.

Brad's eyes widened at her use of the safe word, the word that signaled the end to whatever action he was taking.

"Why do you need to say the safe word? I am not doing anything to you that hurts you." He was truly perplexed.

"Play is over if I say the word, right?"

"Yes." Brad was watching her with a surprised look in his eyes, but he had stopped stroking his cock.

"Well, I am done playing. I am not your slave and you are not my master. I cannot say those words. It is difficult enough to have to call you 'sir' every time I open my mouth in here."

"I thought you wanted and needed to give up control."

"Giving up control is one thing. Mixing pain with pleasure is a part of what I want. Even spanking works for me, but not like tonight. Not like I am some creature who needs to be cuffed to learn her place. And I am no man's slave. Sex partner, yes. Role-playing, yes. Begging, no. No man is my master. No one." Kat's voice was rising. "I've reached my limit. Thank you for teaching me that, Brad. But, I can't do this anymore. I just can't."

Brad stood and moved toward her. She instinctively cringed back. That gesture told both of them more than her words could say. "I'm not going to hurt you, Kat. I would never hurt you. I was just going to help you to your feet."

He reached out his hand. She grasped it, and he pulled her up. He truly looked astonished at her outburst. Kat just shook her head and moved toward the clothes she had left on the chair.

She dressed in silence, and he did the same.

"Please, Kat, reconsider. We can take a few steps back before we move forward again. Perhaps I just pushed you along too fast."

"I can't, Brad. Knowing that ultimately you need this level of domination over me will make me defy you and that will make you crazy. You want more from me than I can give, more than I want to give. The sex was amazing. You're a good man, but just not the man for me. And I am not the woman for you."

OUT OF CONTROL: KAT'S STORY

For the last time, Kat stepped out of the room that had been her sexual sanctuary. Putting on her coat felt like putting on her own skin again. She looked around Brad's apartment; it had been a refuge for her. But she did not need to hide any longer; Kat had found herself. Brad made no move to stop her as she opened the door to the silent marble hallway of the church. "Good-bye, *Sir.*"

CHAPTER FOURTEEN

The ringing was making her crazy. Kat's nerves were frayed, and her temper kept flaring at even the smallest annoyance. So she was getting really pissed at the ringing phones that kept interrupting her quiet Sunday afternoon, the latest in a long stretch of lazy Sunday afternoons. By last count, her house phone had rung three times and her cell phone was now ringing for the fourth time. It was not her grandmother, her parents or her brothers calling. It wasn't Mia or Zack but it was a local number that kept popping up as she screened each call. *That is it! Enough already!* Kat angrily punched the answer key and almost shouted into her cell phone.

"Hello! Who the hell is this?"

"If you answered your damn e-mail or your damn phone once in a while, you would know who the hell it is!" Zack's voice was loud and clear. And sounded very pissed.

"How was I supposed to know this was you? This is not your cell or home or office number." Kat was not going to apologize for not answering a strange number.

"Well it's my new number, which you would know if you were not hiding out in the land of the living dead. Why the hell haven't you been in touch? It's been over a month. It's fucking March already. It's almost Passover. It's almost goddamn spring!"

"I have been busy at work. I haven't been on the computer at home. It was too cold to go to the gym after work. You could have left me a voice message that you were changing your number. Then I would have known this was you."

OUT OF CONTROL: KAT'S STORY

"I left you over a dozen voice messages and texts in February. Your damn mailbox is full." He was right, Kat had to concede. She had just shut down after she walked out of Brad's apartment. It was not that she missed him or even regretted her decision to end their relationship, such as it was. She had just needed some time to figure out how and why she had let someone take so much control over life.

"Well, you have my attention now. What is so goddamn important that you needed to harass me with a gazillion phone calls and everything else?"

"Harass you? I ought to spank your ass for you. You've had everyone worried with your 'I'm too tired, I'm too busy' act. Your grandmother had to ask me if you were coming for the first night of Passover. No man is worth making Bubbe worry about whether you would be at the Seder, I don't care how *tall, dark and handsome* he is."

A sudden wash of shame at how she had ignored her beloved grandmother swept over Kat. She disguised her guilt with irritation. "Oh, I should have known that you and Mia would put your heads together about me again. How much did she tell you this time?" *Damn, Mia.* Kat had explained to her friend some of the reasons she had stopped seeing Brad, but had kept the kneeling and all that out of the conversation. In the telling, it had lost its eroticism and was just embarrassing. *And now Mia had told Zack about Brad! Damn!*

"Mia only said that you were seeing some guy you described as *tall, dark and handsome* back in December and January and that it was all hot and heavy. And then, suddenly, around the end of January: nothing. You were done with him. And you were shutting down. Again." Some of the concern Kat had unintentionally caused crept into Zack's voice. Kat felt a twinge of guilt at worrying her friends.

"I didn't shut down, I just needed some time to think. Jeez, it's not like I was after Michael." Kat could not even remember the six months after Michael had died, and except for work, most of the next year had been a blur, too.

"No? Well, I'm glad to hear it," Zack snapped back at her. After a pause, his voice softened slightly. "Anyway, get your jacket and rubber boots on and meet me out front in fifteen minutes. It's chilly and muddy as all hell where we're going."

"I don't want to go out this afternoon. Why should I?" Kat was so exasperated with him. *Had he not been listening to me?*

"Because I said so." And his phone shut down.

Kat sat staring at her phone. She was not going with him anywhere. *Who does he think he is to order me around?* Deep inside her was a shimmer of...something. *Curiosity*, she told herself. She was just wondering where he was taking her, that was all. But, if she was honest with herself, she would have to admit that a little thrill had shot through her when he had gotten all bossy and...domineering. *No, wait, stop. It's Zack. It's just Zack. But didn't he say something about spanking?*

Still, she quickly rose, went to the front closet and pulled out the boots she wore when she went to the family farm. Tucking her jeans into the tall green Wellingtons, she wrapped her neck in a plaid scarf and reached for her old tan barn jacket. She was *not* going to dress up for him. Kat threw her keys, cell phone and ancient brown leather gloves into the jacket's roomy pockets and hurried out to the elevator.

A brisk March wind lifted off the Hudson and swirled through the streets of Downtown Troy. Kat huddled deeper into her jacket and wished she had worn more than a camisole under the bulky knit sweater she had put on that morning. At least her feet were warm enough. *Where the hell is Zack?* She craned her next for a better look down Third Street, trying to pick his Lexus out of the line of cars waiting at the light. A shiny navy blue Porsche Cayenne pulled to the curb in front of her. The tinted window slid down silently and there was Zack.

"Hop in, you look like you're freezing to death."

Kat just stood there with her mouth hanging open. What was cosmopolitan Zack doing in a rough-and-tumble vehicle like the one she was staring at?

OUT OF CONTROL: KAT'S STORY

He leaned over and opened the passenger door for her. "Get in, Katarina, before your mouth is frozen wide open. You look like a frog!"

That last insult was enough to galvanize her. Within moments, she was in her seat and they were pulling away from the curb.

"Is this yours? Where is your Lexus? When did you get this? *Why* did you buy an SUV?"

"It's mine. I bought it a few days ago, and it isn't an SUV, it's a Porsche. And I bought it because I need it."

"Why could you possibly need an SUV, even a Porsche SUV? To drive up to Lake Placid to ski once a season? To get across the bridge between downtown Troy and downtown Albany?" As much as she was loving teasing him, Kat was loving even more the heated leather seats, the sound system and the smooth power of the vehicle as it climbed Hoosick Street and took them out of Troy.

"I needed it to get out of town, to get out here." Zack turned off Hoosick and headed toward the hill towns.

Kat just sat silently, watching the countryside, the muddy fields giving way to slopes that were still covered in snow. At the top of a slight rise in the road, Zack made a right between two stone pillars. The driveway wound through some ancient oak trees and then the house came into view. It was mammoth!

"Whose house is this?" Kat exclaimed as he pulled up in front on the brick circular driveway. She could see a three-car garage off to the side of the stately pale yellow stucco home. The entrance featured a tall wrought iron double door, flanked by clay pots filled with small evergreens. Snow-covered slopes gently rolled away from the house, dotted with mature trees and what looked like raised flowerbeds, still buried under a blanket of white.

Zack put the Cayenne in Park and turned off the engine. He opened the driver's door and stepped out. As he slammed the door, he said, simply, "It's mine."

Kat was out of her seatbelt in a flash, before Zack could open the passenger door.

"It's yours?" She all but shrieked. "What the hell do you mean, 'It's mine'?"

"Calm down. Just because you decide to hibernate for almost six weeks doesn't mean the rest of us stopped living, too. Come with me," he took her arm and led her to the tile-covered porch that swept across the entire front of the house. "I'd like to show it to you."

Kat was too astonished to argue. The doors opened into a two-story high foyer, well lit by a massive wrought iron chandelier that reflected off the creamy white of the marble floor. It was the type of house that would leave most people speechless.

But, not Zack. As if he were a real estate agent showing the house to a rich prospective client, he led her from the entry to the living room, through the formal dining room to a chef's kitchen—pointing out the restaurant-quality appliances, the butler's pantry—the powder room (the size of her bedroom, Kat noted to herself), the family room with its floor-to-ceiling windows overlooking the brick patio, the in-ground pool, the koi pond and orchards in the distance. Some of the rooms held furniture obviously selected to fill the huge spaces.

"I bought some of the furniture from the previous owners; certain rooms, like the library, had been designed specifically for the furniture. And as it was a bank sale, they were happy to get whatever they could for it." They were back in the family room.

"How did you find this place?" Kat could not believe that in four, maybe six weeks, Zack had found, purchased and had the closing on a property this expensive.

"You remember me complaining this summer about dating real estate agents? Well, the woman I was referring to called me in November to tell me that the perfect country house for me was back on the market and could be had for a song. It belonged to one of the cronies of the former Governor, you know, one of his minions involved in the land and horses deal last year. Seems he couldn't make the mortgage payment once he lost his government contracts, and he had mounting legal fees. The price was reduced, then reduced again. Really, like my Long Island grandmother used to say, 'it was such a deal.'"

"Still Zack, it must have cost a small fortune. I know you've done well, but this house represents a serious investment. Are you sure you can afford it?" Overwhelmed by the magnitude of the house, Kat could not imagine how her friend managed it.

"Thank you for your concern, Kat, but I'm fine. You know I inherited some money when my mother passed away, some of that Long Island money that her parents had left her. And, the firm has done very well in the past few years, since the Scotto murder trials." Zack stood framed by the windows that afforded a view of at least half of Rensselaer County. He looked like a country squire, standing there in his leather jacket, sweater and jeans. Strangely, Kat thought, he looked like he belonged there.

"I still can't believe you are out here in the country. You are just about ten minutes from the family farm. You and Nate are practically neighbors." She eyed him accusingly. "You never wanted to leave the city. You know, there is no pizza delivery out here, don't you?"

"Actually, there is and there's a Chinese restaurant that delivers, too." Zack laughed.

"Well, there's no gym. That will make you crazy."

"Let me show you the floor below this." Zack took her hand and escorted her across a short hallway and down a flight of stairs. The lower level opened onto another patio with a hot tub and a path to the pool. The room that included the requisite pool table, big screen television and juke box featured an oak bar that would have done any pub downtown proud. There were stools at the bar, a few round tables with pub chairs and a comfortable sectional covered in deep red leather. Off to the right was a double doorway that opened into a home theatre, with two levels of recliners and a floor to ceiling movie screen. Kat started laughing in disbelief when Zack turned her to walk down the hall on the left that opened into a state-of-the-art gym, complete with a sauna and a huge bathroom featuring a walk-in shower large enough to hold four people.

Kat sat down on one of the weight benches, shaking her head. "Zack, I am at a loss for words. I had no idea you were even thinking of moving away from downtown. I had no idea that you were looking for a country house or had found one. That you could afford a property like this is news to me, too. What kind of friend am I who is so oblivious to what is going on in your life? I am so sorry that I wasn't present enough to share this whole experience with you. But, I still can't figure out what you are going to do with all this space."

Zack sat down beside her and took her hands in his. "I'm getting married."

CHAPTER FIFTEEN

Kat thought she might faint. She could almost feel the color drain from her face and her eyes roll back in her head. Katarina simply stared at Zack, tears gathering in her widening violet eyes.

"Married?" Her voice was a raspy whisper. Kat was surprised she had any breath at all, given the knife of pain that had pierced her heart at Zack's statement. *Married. Zack? She had no words left.* She could not bring herself to ask him who he was marrying; it didn't matter, no one could possibly be good enough for Zack. But he was her friend, so she had to at least feign happiness for him, even though she was drowning in unshed tears.

"Mazel tov. Who's the lucky lady?" *Which one of his lady friends has landed him?* Oh, God, she hoped it wasn't the opera singer!

"You really *are* hopeless, Katarina. I'm going to marry you." He lifted her hands to his lips and kissed them. The touch of his mouth sent a shiver down her spine.

"Me?" This time she did squeak.

"Yes, you. I figured I better snatch you up before you fell under the control of some true Dom and you were lost to me forever. Your recent taste in men, if you don't mind me saying, has really gone from bad to worse."

Well, now she was getting pissed. Kat's cheeks flushed red, and she jerked her hands from his. "Who do you think you are? Telling me that my taste in men sucks, telling me we are going to get married. Not that I would have you, but you didn't even ask me."

"I don't have to ask you, Katarina. From now on, you are going to do as you are told. At least in matters of the heart. And matters of the pussy and the cock, too." Zack's elegant hands grasped her wrists, shackling them with his fingers. Kat gasped at his coarse language, she did not think she had ever heard Zack say *cock* or *pussy* before.

"What are you talking about, Zack? You and I have never been, you know, that way, together. We're friends, you know that, just friends." If they were just friends, she thought, why were her hands shaking from his touch? Why were those delicious little frissons of passion shooting from her nipples to her pussy? Why was she staring at his mouth as if seeing it for the first time, wondering how it would feel on her lips, her breasts and her clit?

Zack was shaking his head at her, as if she were some backward schoolgirl. "Katarina, we are friends. We could only be friends because Michael found you first. I fell in love with you the moment he introduced us, and I have never stopped loving you."

"You never said anything. You never showed me anything other than platonic affection and friendship."

"How could I? You were in love with my best friend. You were married to my best friend. And then he died and you fell in love with his memory. How could I intrude on that? It was as if you had died too." Zack shook his head, sadly. "So I just loved you, I was content just loving you. But then you started to come back to life. You have no idea how crazy you made me."

He tightened his grip on her wrists, shaking them to emphasize his words. "You have no idea what hell it was to know you were having sex with other men, men who did not love you, could not love you the way I did. But, you needed to find yourself. You needed to discover who you were, what you needed. You needed to realize what I have known about you since the beginning, what even Michael did not know. You need to be controlled."

"Stop! Stop it!" Katarina pulled away from him. "You don't mean any of this. You're just saying this because you and Mia think I am broken by what happened with Brad. You think you need to rescue me like you always have before I get hurt by some man. You don't love me that way. You don't really want me!" She stood.

Zack shot to his feet. One hand grabbed her long braid and pulled her head back so her eyes met his. His other hand pressed on her back, pushing her up against him, so they were touching from chests to knees. Kat saw fury in his face, heard it in his voice, as he spat out the words "I don't love you? I don't want you? You little fool." And then his mouth was on hers, grinding his lips on her lips until they parted and his tongue swept into her mouth, claiming her in a kiss that was both fierce and tender.

She hung there, limp in his grasp. Nothing that had come before had prepared her for Zack's kiss. It was like discovering an entire new universe, a universe that was home.

He tasted of mint and passion. His body was rock hard against hers, she could feel his erection pressing into her belly, through their jackets, through their jeans. She could hear a woman moaning and realized the needy sound was coming from her.

Zack broke the kiss. They stood facing each other, chests heaving as they strove to drag air into their lungs. Zack's hands reached up to frame her face. "Say it. Say yes. Say you are going to marry me." He bent to kiss her again.

"Stop. Stop! *Safety!*"

He pulled his face away, a sardonic look in his eyes.

"*Safety?* Are you pulling some sort of safe word on me? For just a kiss? What the hell have you been playing at with these guys?"

"You weren't listening to me. I just thought you might if you heard an unfamiliar word."

"Unfamiliar? You think I don't know what safe words are used for?"

"Well, I don't know what you know and what you don't, do I? I want you to listen to me." When he nodded, now vaguely amused with her, she continued. "I love you, Zack. I've always loved you, I thought just as a friend. But when you said you were getting married, and I thought it was to someone else, it hurt. It hurt so bad that I knew I must love you because I hurt so much at the thought of you marrying anyone but me."

He made a move to kiss her again but again Kat stopped him. "No, I haven't said I will marry you. Not yet. I've changed this past year; even you noticed it. I'm not the same girl you met in law school. I'm not the same woman who married Michael. I'm not even the same woman who dated Sam and Rick and Bradley." She took a deep breath. "I'm not a submissive, and I don't want a master to dominate me. But, I do want more than just, you know, regular sex." Now she was blushing, and he was grinning.

"Let me see if I understand. You won't say yes to my proposal unless I agree not to dominate you in the bedroom. But you want me to control you, don't you? You want a little pain with your pleasure, don't you? You want to play with toys, and restraints, and clamps, but you don't want to be a sex slave. Am I right?" Zack's smile was gone.

"I don't want to be made to beg, I don't want to kneel and I don't want to have to fucking say *sir* every time." The words burst from her lips.

Zack sighed as if it was taking all the control he had in the world to speak to her in a normal voice. "All right, Katarina, come with me. When we are finished, I expect you to give me an answer to my proposal. Yes or no, I will abide by your decision. Agreed?"

Kat nodded her agreement. Zack took her hand and led her back to the bar area. Off to the side was a small elevator she had not noticed on their initial inspection. Within moments, they had been whisked to the top floor of the mansion. Zack practically dragged her down the hall to two white double doors. Pushing them open, he revealed a master bedroom suite larger than her entire apartment. A beautiful Oriental carpet covered the dark hard wood floors. The only pieces of furniture in the room were an enormous four-poster bed against the far wall with a heavily embroidered canopy and curtains, held in place by thick ivory silk cords. At the foot of the bed sat an intricately carved antique trunk. Kat had seen that trunk in the bedroom of Zack's condo in Troy.

"Take off your coat and boots, Kat. Leave them by the door." Zack tossed his jacket near the door and kicked off his shoes. She did the same, dropping her coat on top of his then pulling off her boots. They stood facing each other, clad in their heavy sweaters, jeans and thick wool socks. He pulled his sweater over his head, letting it fall. Kat hesitated so he grabbed her sweater at the hem and pulled it up and off. Zack's breath caught at the sight of Kat's breasts, cupped in the stretchy cotton camisole, her nipples rosy and hard in the cool air.

Jeans were next, first Zack's then Kat's. She was in soft white cotton; Zack was in dark gray boxers. And he was wearing those stupid gray wool socks that he and Michael had shared.

A small sob escaped her lips. Zack's eyes followed her gaze to his feet. He reached for both her hands, and held them gently in his own.

"Don't, Kat. Don't feel sad. We both loved him and he loved us. I have to believe that he would want us to be happy."

Kat knew he was right. She realized she could believe this because Zack was telling her.

And suddenly she could feel the weight of Michael's loss lift from her heart. She could still love him and love the beautiful man standing before her, because Zack loved her and he loved Michael.

Then she smiled, a pure, sweet smile. Zack swept her up and into his arms for a deep kiss. He swung her toward the bed, his lips never leaving hers and gently laid her across the satin duvet cover.

He lay down beside her. Then their hands were everywhere. Kat could not get enough of the feel of the crisp brown hair that lightly covered his chest, her fingernails scraping across his hard male nipples. Zack was soon tugging the camisole off her, revealing pale white breasts tipped with deep rose nipples. He teased them to aching peaks with his fingers and then his mouth.

Zack rolled on top of her, resting between her long legs, propped on his elbows, kissing her deeper and deeper. Her nipples, abraded by the hair on his chest, were throbbing with need. Then he broke the kiss, taking each of her hands and pulling her arms up. Quickly, saying nothing, only flashing that devilish grin, he had her wrists secured by the silken ties on the bedpost. Then he bent to lave her nipples with his clever tongue, nipping at them until she was practically purring.

Sliding down Kat's body, Zack took her simple white cotton panties with him. He gasped in surprise at the sight of her cleanly shaved pussy. He looked back up at her, a question in his eyes.

"Well, hmmm, well, Brad. Brad liked me to have no hair there so he would shave me once a week." Zack's eyebrows shot up. "So, when we ended and the hair started to grow back," Kat was blushing furiously now, "it itched. So, I just decided to keep it bare. When Denise does my haircut, instead of a bikini wax like I used to get, I just get the whole thing waxed. So it doesn't itch, you see?" Her voice squeaked that last out.

"You can stop that. If you want it bare, and I have to say this is an unexpected and very intriguing development, I will shave you. Your pussy is going to belong to me and only me."

Kat shivered at his words. Then grinned and whispered naughtily, "Yes, *sir.*"

Zack's response was to take her ankles in his hands. He soon wrapped them in silk cords, leaving her wide open to him. He ran a finger down her slit, capturing the honey that was already dripping from her. He put his finger to his lips and sucked. An arrow of desire shot straight to Kat's clit.

His eyes locked on hers, Zack pulled off his boxers and came to stand next to the bed. His cock was perfectly cut and very thick. A drop of cum pearled at its tip. Zack caught the silky liquid on his thumb then smeared it on Kat's lips. She lapped it up like the kitten that she was.

"Do you like the taste? Do you want some more?"

She nodded yes.

"Do you want to suck my cock as much as I want to eat your pussy?"

Kat vigorously nodded her head in the affirmative.

"Well, I don't want to wait, *ketzele*. Let's do this together."

Before she knew what was happening, Zack had climbed back up on the bed. He swung a leg over her outstretched arms and head so that his cock was dangling just above her lips as he straddled her face. He buried his face in her crotch, his clever fingers spreading her pussy lips. The touch of his tongue on her clit made her buck, forcing it further into his mouth. His tongue swept around her nub and then he began to suck her.

Kat's head fell back. Zack's cock brushed her lips. She opened her mouth and licked the slick head of his cock, running her tongue around and around it. He lowered his cock just an inch as he continued to eat her pussy. Kat caught it and held the head delicately between her teeth as her tongue continued to lick him. Then she arched her neck and sucked him into her mouth. He answered her by biting gently on her clit as he slid one finger into her pussy. She thrust her mound against his mouth; Zack slid his cock as far down her throat as it would go.

It was overwhelming to her. Each movement Kat made with her pussy, Zack imitated with his cock. A twin caress from Zack's mouth and tongue answered each caress of Kat's mouth or tongue. Intense pleasure built quickly. Kat could feel the first waves of the orgasm rippling through her. She sucked Zack's cock harder and harder as it pumped in and out of her mouth. His fingers were fucking her with the same rhythm, his mouth never leaving her pussy.

The explosion ripped through her, her hips bucking and grinding against his mouth. He held her ass in his hands, eating up the last drop of honey that gushed from her slick passage.

Before he could come in her mouth, Zack lifted himself off her and rolled to his side. Then he was rummaging in the trunk. Packets of condoms fell on the floor. Waiting for him to sheath himself, Kat lay gasping for breath, her lips swollen and glistening from the cum that had escaped from his cock. He pulled a pillow from the head of the bed and propped her hips up at an angle. He kissed her deeply, their tongues dancing, tasting each other, before he settled himself between her legs.

Watching her, he took forever sliding into her. Zack's cock was so thick that it filled her, stretching her vagina, until buried within her. He pulled almost all the way out of her and then slid back in, to the hilt. This time as he settled inside her, he took her breasts in his hands and squeezed. Her vagina contracted around his penis. Still squeezing her breasts, he slid halfway out then back in, as his fingers pinched her nipples. Answering spasms clutched his cock as he moved in her, in and out, torturing her nipples with each thrust.

Her orgasm was building; wave after wave of pleasure followed each stab of pain. Kat was writhing on the bed, her limbs pulled taut by the restraints, limiting her movements, but intensifying the pressure building within her. Zack was the master of restraint, never varying the speed or depths of his thrusts, just fucking her and fucking her until finally, in a voice, rough with need, Kat pleaded with him to make her come.

"Please, please, Zack. Oh, God, please now. *Now.* Yes, *Yes!*" He was buried deep within her, moving faster and faster. His hands left her breasts. Delving between them, he found her throbbing nub and pressed against it. Her back arched off the bed, her head whipped from side to side as he drove into her one last time and came. She fell back, and he collapsed next to her.

They sucked in deep breaths as if they had just run a marathon.

After a few moments, Zack loosened the cords, and she slipped her hands and feet out of the restraints. Kat rolled to him, resting her head on his chest, as his arms wrapped around her. He kissed her damp forehead. Kat smiled and nudged his chin with her nose. He drew back his head to look down at her. "What?" he asked when he saw the light in her eyes.

"Yes."

CHAPTER SIXTEEN

"Did you just agree to marry me because I fucked your brains out and you are not thinking straight or do you really mean it?" Zack had tilted Kat's face up to his.

"Well," she drawled, "that was pretty amazing sex, *tatala*. And I would hate to think we were only going to do it once, so, yes, the sex is part of the reason I just accepted your proposal." Kat searched Zack's face for a sign of what he was feeling, but he was wearing his poker face so she found no clues. "And, of course, this amazing house. But I said yes because I love you. I love you more than I thought I would ever love anyone again."

"You made me wait long enough for you, Kat. Damn, ten long years." He gave her braid a rough tug.

"You know what Bubbe says, 'all good things come to those who wait.' And I'm glad you waited. Who knew you had so much patience?" Kat poked a finger at his chest. It felt so good, so right to be in Zack's arms, in the arms of her friend, now her lover, soon to be her husband. She snuggled closer to him, placing a soft kiss where she had just poked his chest.

"Kat, there's something else I have to ask you." Once again, Zack pulled away slightly so he could see her face. "I really want children." Her face lit up at his words. "And I'd like to have them while I am still young enough to play catch with them and take them to ball games and teach them to drive." She smiled. "You know what I mean. So, if you agree, I want to start trying to make a baby as soon as possible."

"We can start today, if you like. I don't want to be fifty and pregnant, you know."

"Well, we should probably get blood tests before we get rid of the condoms, don't you think? There have been a lot of...people...in both our pasts." It was a ridiculous thing to say to the woman you had just proposed to, but Zack had always been practical and cautious.

"I don't know about you, Zack, but I always used condoms *and* I had a blood test after each one of my recent lovers. Maybe you can't say the same." There was no small amount of hurt conveyed in her voice. *How many lady friends had there been for him? How many men did Zack think I had fucked?*

He kissed her hard. "That's my smart, careful Kat. I knew even when you were acting crazy you would still be practical. And I have done the same, so I am just tossing these away." He kicked at some of the wrapped condoms still scattered across the foot of the bed.

"Zack, *tatala*, as long as we are being so honest and practical here, there's something I have to ask you." Zack flushed a bit, looked away, and then returned his gaze to her face.

"Kat, there haven't been that many women I've taken to bed, if that's what you want to know. Probably far fewer than you and Mia figure there have been. Not that I didn't date dozens of women, but I didn't have sex with all of them. I have certain requirements in that area and not everyone met my criteria."

"I wasn't really going to ask about how many women there have been, Zack, though I am relieved to hear that there have not been the number of lady friends that Mia predicted. Our pasts are in the past. Just so long as none of them show up at the door wanting to start up with you again. Then, there will be trouble." Zack laughed and hugged her tighter.

"What I wanted to ask, well, really, discuss with you, was, you know, the sex." Kat could feel the red rising in her cheeks. Zack was staring at her now, with a funny look in his stormy eyes.

"Didn't you like 'the sex'? I could have sworn I heard you screaming my name a few minutes ago."

"Zack, you know I liked it. I loved it. It's just that, well, over the last several months, my tastes have changed a lot, and I've discovered some things I really like and some things I don't like. The sex with you was great, and I loved the silk cords so, I am hoping, you see, that we could continue to use them and, you know, other stuff like that."

"I see. So you are telling me that you like to be tied up or restrained during sex. And I know you like it when I play a little rough, when there is some pain involved. I assume there is more, since you know about safe words. Do you like whips and chains?"

Did he just snicker at the look on my face? Kat thought Zack was finding the conversation way too amusing. And arousing, if his growing erection was any indication.

"No. Well, I don't know but I don't think so. I like, ummm, toys and equipment, you know, like clamps. Do you know what I mean?"

"Yes, *ketzie*, I know exactly what you mean. Scoot off the bed and open that trunk, Katarina." Kat rolled over and moved to the end of the bed. The chest was unlocked, but the top was heavy. She had to lift it up with both hands. Then she looked into the trunk. Gasped. Her nipples hardened. She stared at Zack, who was sitting in the middle of the huge bed, openly laughing now.

"Is this stuff all yours?" Kat was eyeing what looked to be a collection put together by the Marquis de Sade. Clamps of various sizes and materials hung from the satin lining of the trunk lid. Silk cords were coiled in neat piles, next to what looked like whips. Separated from them was a collection of vibrators, dildos and other contraptions she could not identify. And there was leather; she inhaled the rich scent of good leather, mingled with various spicy smells and definitely some citrus. It was a treasure trove of dark delights.

"Some of it is mine, like the handcuffs I got from the detectives in Albany when I left the DA's office. Most of it is new, purchased especially for you."

"Me? How did you know I would like these things?"

"From some of the things you said, but I knew for certain when I saw those bruises on your wrists. That's when I started putting all of this together, Kat. I could never approach you while you were still mourning Michael. When you started dating again, I wanted to make a move but, well, I have certain *things* I like and need, and I was not certain you could accept that side of me even if you could accept that I loved you. Our conversation about those marks opened my eyes about you."

Kat was emboldened by the contents of Zack's trunk and secure after hearing the lengths he had been willing to go to for her. "I can't beg. And I don't care for kneeling, but I can, sometimes. I don't think I would like chains, but these handcuffs are very intriguing." She reached down to take them out, dangling them from her fingers. Zack's cock got even harder. "And I really like the nipple clamps." Kat pulled a pair from the trunk and tossed them on the bed.

"Come here, Katarina. Right here next to the bed so I can put those clamps on your nipples." Zack was using his dark and dangerous voice. Kat's insides were melting. But she didn't move. Not yet. She had one more thing to say to this man who was to control her desires.

"You didn't say anything about spanking, Zack. I don't think I should be punished with spankings. I don't want you to hit me like that. But, if you were to spank me as part of the sex, I think that would be fine."

"Darling, this is your lucky day. Is there an envelope in the trunk? Yes? Good. Open it and read what is inside." Zack had come to stand beside her.

Kat dropped the handcuffs on the bed and read the contents of the envelope. With a gleeful whoop, she was in his arms. As they tumbled onto the bed, the piece of paper drifted to the floor. The certificate of completion issued to Zachary Aaron Reichman from the Manhattan School of Erotic Spanking.

THE END

Dear Reader,

Thank you so much for buying this book. It is my first erotic romance and I hope it will not be the last. In fact, Rick has been clamoring for a book of his own, one last adventure, one more summer on Long Beach Island. And one more lover, who might finally win this warrior's heart. Britt, beautiful and brutalized by the same battles that hardened Rick's heart, has washed up on the Jersey Shore. Will she be the one? I've included an excerpt of *Taking Control: Rick's Story*, coming in 2017.

If you like seasoned romance, I know you will love my contemporary erotic romance, *Unanswered Prayers*. It's summer 2001 and Naomi Stein has been praying for a little peace from her son, her ex-husband and her editor. Instead, she's following surly Country singer Sam Rhodes across the USA, covering his breakout concert tour for Rolling Stone. Sam has had bad luck with women and Naomi is trouble from the start. He tries to keep the feisty, sexy blonde at arm's length...until Naomi gets right in his face. The hottest tour of the summer has just caught on fire. The music gets better and the romance steamier as they criss-cross the country. Will their passion burn out as autumn approaches? Stubborn pride forces them apart until the tragedy of 9/11 compels them to face each other one last time.

I also hope you will like *Cocktales*, a memoir about my adventures as a 50-year-old who ventures into dating online. It is my true-life, almost ten-year romp through lust, love and lies. *Cocktales* is an honest, humorous and hopeful collection for men and women of all ages who wonder if they will ever find someone who wants them.

XOXO

Morgan Malone

ABOUT MORGAN MALONE

Morgan Malone has been reading romance since the age of twelve when she snuck her mother's copy of *Gone with the Wind* under the bed covers to read by flashlight. A published author at the age of eight, she has been writing romance for the last five years, after retiring from a thirty-year career as a judge and counsel at a New York State agency. Morgan lives near Saratoga Springs, NY, with her chocolate Labrador retriever. When not writing erotic romance, Morgan can be found penning her memoirs or painting watercolors. Visit her on Facebook at www.facebook.com/MorganMaloneAuthor/, Twitter at @MMaloneAuthor or her new website, www.morganmaloneauthor.com.

Also available by Morgan Malone:

Shoulder to Lean On
Unanswered Prayers
Cocktales

If you enjoyed Morgan Malone's **Out of Control: Kat's Story**, please consider telling others and writing a review on Amazon or GoodReads.

TAKING CONTROL: RICK'S STORY

The tang of the salt air hit Rick before he saw or even heard the Atlantic Ocean. He rolled down the window of his battered green Jeep and took a deep, cleansing breath. A calm he had not felt in months began to spread through him, almost, but not quite reaching his troubled soul. Nine months since he had been down the Shore. Nine months of running away, nine months of searching.

Springsteen was singing about glory days on the radio. Rick sang along for a few bars then abruptly switched off the radio. His glory days were long behind him. *Not that any of my days were glory days.* Hard to glorify any of the campaigns, missions and damn stupid forays the government had sent him on over the last twenty-five years. Mud, dust, dirt and blood comprised most of his memories. The silence in the Jeep was filled by the crashing of waves and the ocean breeze. Cool air flowed through the window, blowing away the heat and humidity of the July evening, washing some of the bitter regret from Rick's face. He glanced in the rearview mirror before he put on his turn signal to leave the highway and cut toward the shore. The man who stared back at him looked weary and old. The highlights in his strawberry blond hair appeared golden in the light but he guessed it was probably just more gray hair. His dark tan seemed to emphasize the wrinkles that creased his forehead and fanned out from the corners of his eyes. Years of scrunching his eyes from bright sun and fierce winds were embedded in those lines.

Zipping down Long Beach Boulevard, Rick caught a few glimpses of the water between the houses. The moon hung low in the summer sky, casting a glittering path across the waves and brightening the road ahead of him. With a great sigh of relief, Rick turned down First Street, then pulled the dusty Jeep into the sand covered drive of a three story house facing the Atlantic. Built into the dune, the garage faced the street, access to the front of the house was up a flight of wooden stairs. Rick swung his long jean clad legs out of the Jeep. Dusty cowboy boots planted in the drifting beach sand, he paused for a moment. *Home.* Reaching into the back seat, he pulled out a worn green duffel and slung a leather computer case over his shoulder. Traveling light meant only one trip up the long flight of stairs to the ocean-facing deck. He paused by a loose brick to feel around under it for his spare key. *Hmmm, not precisely where I left it the last time. What's up?*

Easing a pistol from the small of his back, he climbed the deck stairs swiftly and silently. Rick left the duffel and briefcase on the edge of the deck, glanced briefly out at the beach before moving quickly to the French doors to his right. He tried the handle but the door was locked. Shifting the gun to his left hand, he quietly unlocked the door. Nothing in the open living room, dining area and kitchen appeared to be out of place. The room was neat and dust-free because he had called ahead to his cleaning service to prepare the cottage for him, including stocking the fridge and pantry. And wine rack, he noted, as he slipped silently through the room and up the stairs to the second floor. A quick search of the two bedrooms and bathrooms on the upper level revealed nothing and no one.

Still puzzled, with the pistol still in his hand, Rick went back down to the main floor. As he stepped into the living room, he saw a small mahogany box on the couch, weighing down a sheet of heavy grey paper. He recognized the box. He had sent enough of them to grieving parents and spouses. Purple Heart. *Kat.*

A wave of regret swept through him, tugging at a heart he frequently maintained had lost any ability to feel. But, he had come close almost a year ago and his brush with the beautiful and brilliant redhead had sent him running away from the inevitable heartbreak he knew he would cause her.

I guess she took me up on my offer. His last gift to her had been flowers and a note telling her to use the cottage while he was away, noting that he probably would not return until the Fourth of July. The Fourth was hours away, but for a moment he was transported back to the autumn when he had almost fallen in love with the feisty widow of a lawyer/soldier who had died in Iraq ten years earlier. A lawyer who had been blown apart by an IED, just like so many men Rick had known in the past decade. A fate that Rick had narrowly escaped on too many occasions to recall. *I've dodged the bullet too many times. My luck must be damn close to running out. Or it should be.*

He stared at the small box and note for several minutes. Then, sighing and squaring his shoulders, he sat down on the sofa and eased the note out from under the small wooden box. His hands were shaking as he unfolded the heavy grey stationery. The unshed tears in his eyes blurred the bold handwriting.

To Rick. For gallant service above and beyond the call of duty, in honor of all your scars—seen and unseen—this medal is yours. You are an officer and a gentleman—and I will never forget you. Kat

Rick opened the box. *Damn it, Kat. You still know how to get to me.* Inside, resting on velvet, as he knew it would be, was a Purple Heart. Awarded to Kat's late husband posthumously, delivered to Kat by some unremembered officer, accepted with tears and a tremulous smile. And a vacant, sad face that said without words, "What good is this? How will I live without him? I don't want a medal, I want my husband back. But I will take this in his honor and I will hate it and the war that did this to us. And you for being the bearer of this final reminder of how much I have lost." Rick knew. He had delivered such medals to grieving widows, sorrow-stricken mothers, and bereft fathers. Until the day, long ago, when he had gone silent, had disappeared into the secret society of warriors who went unmentioned, unnoticed and with nothing but a helmet sitting on a pile of stones to mark their passing.

For the first time in many years, Rick hung his head and wept.

Made in the USA
Middletown, DE
20 October 2023

41169216R00109